THE
WARM SIDE
— OF THE —
ISLAND

THE

WARM SIDE
— OF THE —
ISLAND

Dixie Burrus Browning

FULL-SERVICE   BOOK-MAKERS

ESTD.   1999

Front cover photograph by Michael Halminski

Copyright © 2019
Dixie Burrus Browning

Published by
The Chapel Hill Press, Inc., Chapel Hill, NC
Originally published by Avalon Books, an imprint of
Thomas Bouregy and Company, Inc. in 1978

ISBN 978-1-59715-198-6
Library of Congress Catalog Number 2019938396

First Printing
Printed in the United States of America

A Note from the Publisher

Welcome back to Cape Hatteras Chronicles!

The Warm Side of the Island is the first book published by Dixie Burrus Browning. With a young adult reader in mind, Dixie began her career as a novelist under the name "Zoe Dozier." The name comes with a big dose of Hatteras Island history. Dixie chose the name "Dozier" because it was the middle name of her grandfather, Captain Ethelbert Dozier Burrus, who sailed in the East Coast and West Indies trade.

This story, just like *Seaspell* and *Warfield Bride*, will lead you down the sandy paths of a Hatteras Island in days gone by. Always a mix of fact and fiction, the books of the Cape Hatteras Chronicles capture a time and place precious to all who have Hatteras in their blood as well as to those who found Hatteras by chance.

Earlier titles in the Cape Hatteras Chronicles:

Seaspell by Bronwyn Williams

Warfield Bride by Bronwyn Williams

Edwina D. Woodbury
Chapel Hill Press

CHAPTER ONE

The North Carolina wind that pressed the windbreaker against her body was cooler than the surging white water that broke about her legs, and Kendrik Haynes took another step and then another until the incoming waves covered her tanned knees and splashed up on the torn-off jeans that barely showed beneath her jacket. The lilac scarf that had held her long, sun-streaked hair had long since blown away, pursued for a while by Charlie, the huge Chesapeake Bay retriever, who had soon returned to the more exciting game of challenging seagulls.

Gradually the rhythm of the surf became a part of her consciousness, and she found herself thinking in tune with the Atlantic. The incoming waves brought energy and new determination; the outgoing, spent waves became remnants of her past that had no place in the new life she meant to make for herself.

Out went Scott with his ideas of the new morality, his facile charm and rather striking good looks.

In came an opportunity to put down new roots in old territory, to build a nest in the tiny cottage willed to her by her grandfather on this small island where she had spent the happiest days of her life.

Out went any pretense of a home with her father and his second wife, now headed for the West to resettle in his wife's hometown.

In came a few months of loafing and beachcombing before looking for a job, of relaxing after an arduous four years at the university.

Out went a close friendship with the two girls she had roomed with at school, for she had no illusions about maintaining ties with the two newly married couples who had moved to New York to try their luck together.

She shivered as the late evening sun dropped beneath the white-capped waters behind her. The chill she felt went deeper than the skin, went down into the very depths of her heart and found a loneliness she had not admitted to herself before. Sally and Edward, Emmy and Keith, Papa and his new bride Grace—but nobody and Kendrik. No Scott, no Grandy, the old man who had been far closer to her than his son-in-law, her own father, had ever been.

She had lost sight of Charlie until she saw him jumping excitedly and circling a tall, angry-looking man who was brushing sand from his clothes and yelling something about an undisciplined monster.

"Get this...damned...away from me!" And something about the law! The angry words were spoken in a deep, harsh voice interspersed with the excited barking of the dog and the raucous cries of the gulls.

"Charlie! Behave yourself!" Kendrik sped over the few yards of sand separating her from the agitated pair. "He doesn't usually carry on like this. I'm sorry he's bothered you. He doesn't mean anything by it. I've never known him to be—" Her placating voice tapered off as she brushed the windblown hair from her eyes and saw him clearly for the first time. The man was taller than most, handsomer by far than most, and definitely angrier than most men she had encountered in her twenty-two years. For some reason, the arrogant cast of his bronzed head and the temper blazing from his deep-set blue eyes set off a spark that ignited her own temper, and she snapped at him.

"Don't be such a nitwit! Chessies aren't vicious, and he probably wouldn't even bark at you if you didn't keep standing there like a beanpole, waving your arms and shouting at him!"

The furious man reached a hand in Kendrik's direction but looked at Charlie and reconsidered. "If you don't haul this mangy-looking mutt away from here, I won't be responsible for his safety, or yours, either!"

Kendrik was stunned. Bad manners were one thing, but this was outright hostility. Never in her life had she witnessed such a display. Usually people responded to her quite differently. Men always were impressed by her rather offbeat looks. Green eyes emphasized by dark brows and thick, brown lashes were not that common, and when they rode at an angle above high-winged cheekbones, the impression made on most men was immediate and favorable.

Speechless with rage at this man's harsh attack, Kendrik let her smoldering glare speak for her for a full minute before she grabbed Charlie's collar and turned away. She ran, dragging the disorderly mass of wet dog along until he got the idea and galloped off toward the ramp on the dunes. Kendrik didn't pause until she reached the top of the sandy ramp, then something compelled her to stop and look back. He was standing as she had left him. From this distance she couldn't see his face, but she had the distinct impression he was looking back at her.

Her anger faded slowly, to be replaced by puzzlement. She turned away and stood for a moment on the high vantage point. Toward the west was the wide, shallow expanse of the Pamlico Sound. To her left, the salt haze hanging in the air marked the turbulence of the inlet, hidden beyond the low shrubs, the wind-sculpted live oaks, and the scattering of small houses that made up the village. Behind her now, the Atlantic was already showing signs of autumn restlessness.

Kendrik slithered down the dune to the paved

drive-out where her little Bluebird waited with all the patience of any fourteen-year-old sedan. She loaded Charlie in and coaxed the engine to start.

Turning right, she headed north on the narrow strip of blacktop, her eyes on the distant woods that sheltered her four-room cottage. As the familiar scenery sped by, her mind returned to the summers past when she had roamed the sandhills and salt marshes, sometimes alone and sometimes with the island children. Her father had spent his vacations fishing or helping Grandy refurbish decoys and mend nets. Mama had wandered the shores with her watercolors, oblivious of anyone else.

Seven years ago the pattern had changed. After Mama had died, Kendrik had clung closer to her grandfather, choosing to spend her holidays with him rather than with Papa, who had retired even deeper into his books.

Then Papa had remarried, and Grace Haynes had forced the breaking of ties when she insisted on taking her new husband to her Texas home for their holidays. There had never been any question of Kendrik's joining them, for few women want a grown stepdaughter foisted on them, and Grace was no exception.

Charlie's excited lunging about in the backseat brought Kendrik's mind back to the present in time to turn off the blacktop into the narrow, winding drive that led to the cottage.

After shaking the sand from Charlie's rug and tossing it under the back porch, she drew him a bucket of fresh water. Then, running up the wooden steps, she unlocked the door and entered the cozy, shingled house, only to groan at the sight of piles of bags, boxes, and instrument cases. Oh, well...first things first! Charlie needed his supper and so did she. After that would be time enough to begin to cope with settling in.

Later on, as she sipped the hot, canned soup, she looked around the room. Pine paneled walls, rag rugs on the floor, surf rods in a rack on one wall, and several of her mother's paintings ... it was truly home. It was the only place that was all hers, a gathering together of things and memories that were of value to her. Soon her own stoneware cooking pots, her ceramic goblets and tea things from various craftsmen's fairs would fill the shelves in the kitchen. Her big basket of quilting scraps would definitely go beside the rocker, her crocheting under the end table, and her books wherever she found room. Musical instruments would probably be propped up in all the corners, ready to be picked up and played as the notion took her.

Kendrik had studied anthropology at the university, but her studies in that and in philosophy and history had been spiced with several courses in folk music. The amiable preoccupation of both her parents during her childhood had left her largely to her own ends, and she had turned to music as a natural substitute for companionship. She had picked up the guitar as a child and played well. After her mother's death, she had bought a banjo and later on a fiddle and had practiced for aching, nonthinking hours until the worst of the grief had gone.

Then there was her recorder. This was her "walking music." Little caring for the amused glances sent her way by others, she had frequently walked the sidewalks and paths of the small university town piping whimsical tunes on the instrument, which fitted quite nicely into her handbag when not in use. Little wonder that with her beguiling music, her spontaneous smile, and her unpretentious beauty, she was unused to encountering enmity.

Kendrik's thoughts slipped back to the man on the beach. He was obviously not a native. his speech alone set him apart. It was a northern accent, educated, despite the rough edges of anger. He didn't have the look of the island families, either. She had to admit that the sharp planes and angles of his features went together in a rather devastating manner, but Lord! That temper!

She dismissed him from her mind and began putting away all her worldly possessions.

CHAPTER TWO

The next several days fell into a pattern that might have proved boring to some members of Kendrik's generation. Mornings were spent scrubbing, painting, and generally refurbishing the cottage. Afternoons belonged to Charlie. Together they roamed for miles along the edges of the sound, picking their way through patches of sharp-edged saltwater grass and piles of dried seaweed, and along the wide, sandy ocean front. There were enriching hours spent walking through the woods surrounding the cottage: the tall, long-leafed pines that filtered the wind so musically, the gnarled live. oaks, the bay laurel, the red-berried holly and yaupons.

Evenings were spent trying different ways of cooking the fish she picked up at the waterfront each day. She played her instruments and read well into the night.

It was a healing time. The last few weeks at the university had been filled with partings that had bruised her far more than was apparent at the time.

The splitting up of three friends who had shared so much had not been unexpected. Sally and Emmy were excited about job-hunting in New York. Even had they not been newly married, they would have deplored a winter on the little North Carolina island after all the summer visitors had gone, just as Kendrik could not have borne New York, or, indeed, any city, for more than a few days.

Scott had been fun to go out with, at first, in those last few weeks before graduation. It had not occurred to her that his feelings were more involved than her own until that last evening. Good looks, too much money, and too much ready charm had not prepared Scott Chandler for rejection by anyone. The basic shallowness of his character was brought more and more to the surface in those last few weeks, and when Kendrik refused to go off alone with him for a week at a mountain resort, it had sparked a scene that had ended the relationship.

"You're a damned prude!" he'd snapped. "If you think you can get me to marry you that way, you've got another thing coming! I'm not about to get tied down!"

Marriage to Scott had never been a part of Kendrik's plans. His company fed the exuberant, fun-loving side of her personality, but it had starved the more sensitive side—the part of her that enjoyed taking fruit, cheese, and wine picnics into the woods for a day spent making music and reading beside a hidden stream, or hunting blackberries or trillium or ground-cedar. Still, something of the bitterness of the parting remained. Kendrik's nature could not accept anger and hostility without withering.

The tense three months after graduation spent helping her father and Grace prepare for the move to Texas had not given her any time to recover from the wounds of those last weeks at the university. The parting with her father had not been bitter, only somehow sad. Rod Haynes was only forty-eight and still an attractive man. He and Kendrik had never been particularly close, but she had loved him and made a great effort to understand when he began to see more and more of Grace Stone soon after his wife died.

Later on, after they had married, they tried to make her feel welcome, but Grace was far too different from her own gentle, easygoing mother for Kendrik ever to feel at home with her. So perhaps it was best, Kendrik told herself, that they had decided to pull up stakes and move West. Grace owned a small ranch in Texas, and Rod

Haynes, a high-school teacher by profession, could easily find a position there.

The parting that had hurt the most was with her grandfather, who had died during her last semester at the university. Kendrik had spent summers with him and Miss Tull, who "did for him," and Charlie, of course, for as long as she could remember. Grandy had taught her to sail after she had helped him build a centerboard into his old flat-bottomed juniper skiff and step a mast. He had showed her his oyster bed and told her where the biggest clams could be found, just below his old bunglow, on the other side of the village.

Clams! Kendrik had not thought of those clams since she arrived last week, but they were there for the taking. The bungalow had had to be sold, after Grandy died. It had been bought by a Marcus Manning, who had arranged for someone to put it into shape for him and Mrs. Manning to move into in October. It was still early in October, so perhaps they weren't there yet. Even if they were, they didn't own the property beyond the shoreline. That was public domain. Anyway, they probably wouldn't care. She would take Charlie and a bucket and go immediately, before the tide came in any higher. That way, she wouldn't even need a clam rake.

She parked the car beside the path leading up to the weathered old house. This was the first time she had come to this part of the village since Grandy had died, and it hurt to look at the familiar shingled bungalow and know that she no longer had any claim to it. Her eyes moved from the shed in the back where they had cleaned fish and shucked clams and oysters, past the fig trees where she had raced with the mockingbirds each morning for the newly ripe sugar figs, to the clothesline by the back porch where they always hung out wet bathing suits.

There was one now! Or rather, a pair of men's trunks and a towel. No other signs of occupation, no car, no sounds coming from inside the house. The windows were open, though.

Oh, well...so they had arrived. If they made a big to-do over her using the path, she would offer Mrs. Manning a few clams.

Looking around for Charlie, she prepared to walk on down to the water when the sight of the Chesapeake running around the corner of the house with a side of fish in his mouth stopped her in her tracks.

"Oh, no!" She ran to the corner around which Charlie had disappeared, dropping her bucket and yelling after him to come back. There was no time to stop before she slammed full tilt into a hard, tall figure coming from the other direction. Instinctively grabbing hold to keep from falling, she looked up into the amazed blue eyes she had last seen staring after her on the beach a week ago.

"You!"

"What the...!" They both gasped at once. She jumped back, cheeks flaming, only to stumble over Charlie, who had crept up silently behind her. Charlie, trying vainly to maintain his hold on the side of fish, let out a yelp. Kendrik landed flat on her back, the wind knocked out of her, and the tall man put back his head and laughed. Laughed!

"Well," he gasped, "I was prepared for high winds. I was prepared for high tides, but nobody prepared me for this mobile calamity...high comedy, you might say!"

Kendrik struggled to sit up, not helped by a rough, wet tongue and a sandy, tentative paw digging at her shoulder. "Oh, go on, Charlie!" she snapped and would have succeeded in sitting up had she not put her hand on the fish Charlie had dropped. This was too much. Angry, embarrassed, frustrated tears spilled over her flushed cheeks, and she swore roundly under her breath. Instantly, the man's laughter stopped, and he knelt beside her.

"Here," he murmured. "You're hurt and I really didn't mean to laugh, but it was too much. . . . You should have seen . . ."

He started to grin again, and Kendrik fumed, "Oh, go chase yourself! Let me alone! You're the most impossible . . . !"

She struggled to her feet and glared up at the deeply tanned face that struggled to contain laughter. Blue eyes that had raged at her on the beach now glinted with amusement, and amazingly enough, it occurred to Kendrik that neither of these was the expression she wanted to see in those eyes, but rather, something much warmer. She stepped back, aghast at the wild, improbable idea.

"I'm sorry about your fish. If you don't mind accepting some clams in exchange I'll bring them by after a while," she muttered, embarrassed and anxious to get away from this disconcerting stranger.

"Where do you get them?" he asked.

Not wishing to prolong the conversation, Kendrik turned away. "Oh, out in the sound," she replied vaguely. "I'll leave you some on the back porch."

"Wait," he commanded. Then, in a milder tone of voice, he said, "I'd really like to go with you. That is, if you don't mind."

What could she say? Yes, I mind? She was chagrined to realize that not only did she not mind, she was actually glad of an opportunity to study this man further. He was unlike anyone she had met before. Or perhaps she just hadn't noticed men of this age—early thirties, she estimated. There was a sureness, a self-contained quality that was completely missing from the boys she had known at college. An intriguing quality.

"Well, it's not far, if you really do want to go," she admitted. Then, glancing down at his khaki-clad legs, she said, "You may have to wade, and you'll have to go barefooted."

"Fine," he replied and stepped out of his canvas shoes. "Did you have a bucket?"

"Oh, I guess I dropped it." She located the bucket where it had rolled near the corner of the house, whistled for Charlie, and turned toward the water.

Tide flats, uncovered at low water, stretched out for several hundred yards, and Kendrik soon began looking for the telltale keyholes in the sand that indicated the presence of clams. When she spotted her first one, she looked up at her partner.

"This is how you find them at low tide. Just dig with your toes, then pick them up." She proceeded to demonstrate.

"Here, I'll take the bucket," he said, reaching for it. As their fingers met on the wire handle, Kendrik was acutely aware of his touch. She glanced up at the man through her thick lashes, wondering if he had felt the same reaction, but he seemed completely impervious to her. To cover her self-consciousness, she stammered, "I—I don't even know your name. Mine's Kendrik—Kendrik Haynes."

"Marcus Manning," he introduced himself. "I'm afraid I owe you an apology, Miss Haynes."

"Oh, no," Kendrik said. Oh, no, she thought. Mr. and Mrs. Marcus Manning.

"I really shouldn't have yelled at you last Tuesday on the beach," he said.

Last Tuesday? He remembered the day, too? Don't be

stupid, warned the stern monitor in her head, but it didn't prevent a warm glow from spreading over her body.

"I had fallen asleep on the beach after hassling over a pretty upsetting situation, and when your dog tried to bury me like an oversized bone, I guess I overreacted. I really am fond of dogs, believe it or not. I guess I just needed something to yell at about then, and you happened along."

He smiled down into eyes that reflected the deep green of the sound. "I'm ashamed to admit that after you left, I saw the fiddler crab hole your dog had been digging out when his excavation threatened to bury me." He watched the appreciative gleam grow in her eyes.

Kendrik could not know how she appeared to the man at that moment. Her golden, tanned face was warmed by sun-pinked cheeks and cooled by sea-green eyes. Long strands of light brown hair, now streaked by the sunshine, blew across a berry-red mouth that quivered into a smile. As her smile widened, revealing a rather endearing irregularity of white teeth, he suddenly looked away.

As if a cloud had passed over the sun, blocking its warmth, Kendrik was aware of a withdrawal. Of what, she was not quite certain. Her thoughts were chaotic. What's wrong with me? she asked herself. He's a stranger, a bad-tempered, sadistic stranger who laughs at the misfortunes of others.... He's a married man, and I'm acting like a silly schoolgirl with a crush on her teacher! Kendrik hid her embarrassment by turning away.

"Look, there's another keyhole." She dug with her toe, then bent to retrieve the hard-shelled clam. Moving away, searching and digging, she left the clams for the silent man walking behind her to gather.

Charlie splashed by in the nearby shallows, and a lone gull overhead protested their presence. Gradually the serenity of the smooth, wet sand and the mirror of water reflecting a calm, late afternoon sky stilled the turmoil within her, and she looked at her companion and smiled.

"Think we have enough for three?" she asked. "Maybe your wife will make you a chowder."

Marcus picked up a broken clam shell and turned it over in his hand, studying it intently. "I guess you'd better take them all. I'll probably eat out tonight, and it would be a shame to waste them."

"Oh, they keep beautifully!" She turned toward him. "Just cover them with a damp burlap bag and put them in the shade." She stopped, her smile fading as he turned and walked away.

"You keep them," he snapped back over his shoulder.

Kendrik's mouth dropped open in surprise. Of all the rude, ungrateful boors! I guess first impressions don't lie, she chided herself. But for a while he seemed so—so married, you stupid girl, and don't you forget it!

Calling Charlie, she picked up the bucket and walked slowly toward the shore, following the long, slender footprints in the wet sand.

CHAPTER THREE

It was several days later that Kendrik went to the village again. As she pulled up in front of the general store, she thought she caught a glimpse of shaggy, black curls in the backyard of the white frame house next door to Grandy's—to the Mannings', she corrected herself. After loading the trunk of the little Bluebird with groceries, she drove the few remaining feet and turned into the driveway beside the white frame house. Calling out as she approached the front porch, she flung her arms wide as the door opened to reveal a tiny girl of about Kendrik's age with a face full of freckles and a mop of black hair.

"Vonnie!" Kendrik grabbed her, and they danced around in circles, hugging, laughing, both trying to speak at once.

Vonnie O'Neal had been the girl next door whenever Kendrik had visited her grandfather. They had been friends since the first time they met over pails and shovels in the sandy stretch that ran behind both houses. Vonnie had graduated from the local high school, then taken a course in practical nursing. Before she could get settled in a job on the mainland, she was called home to take care of her mother, who had broken her hip.

Since then she had been needed by first one, then another of the island people. The nearest hospital was almost eighty miles away, and the little local clinic was hard put to handle all the cases that came up, especially during the tourist season. Now that she was practically engaged to the youngest Hollis boy, she had given up any notion of leaving.

The two girls—long-limbed, sand-colored Kendrik

15

and the tiny, Irish-eyed, dark-haired Vonnie—spent the morning swinging in the old, squeaking swing on the porch. Kendrik heard all the details, pertinent and otherwise, of Vonnie's progressing courtship with Buck Hollis.

"Oh, Ken, you know how we always thought he was so stuck-up? Well, he was really just embarrassed because he liked me a lot and he thought that I thought he was awful and..." She broke off with a giggle.

After catching up on the news of the various island families, all of them known to her since she was a child, Kendrik dropped an overcasual question into a pool of silence.

"How's your sister Erma these days?"

"Oh, she's pretty much the same, I guess." Vonnie's abbreviated nose wrinkled. "She never writes or visits us anymore. You knew she had a job with a newspaper, didn't you? Has her own apartment and everything." Vonnie's sigh held acknowledgment of the end of her own hopes for a career.

"I'm surprised she didn't end up as a model or a television star or something like that. She was always the most glamorous girl down here," Kendrik said.

"She tried to get hooked up with a TV producer or something like that. In fact, she actually had two short jobs on a morning show, but she wasn't awfully good. She photographed like a dream, though! She was doing interviews, and that was how she got this job with the paper. She meets all sorts of super people!"

For some reason never quite clear to Kendrik, there had always been a mutual antipathy between the oldest O'Neal girl and herself. The fact that Kendrik was several years younger and a friend of Vonnie's didn't seem to change matters.

The morning slipped away in reminiscences of past escapades and news of who had married whom and how many children they had. Finally, as she was leaving, having secured a promise of a visit from her friend sometime soon, Kendrik mentioned the man who had been walking the borders of her mind with annoying persistence.

"I understand you have new neighbors. What are they like?"

"Oh, all right, I guess. I've only seen *him*, but I understand there's a *her*, too. Pity. He's the sort you see in tobacco ads, looking superior and horribly intellectual and just reeking with masculinity!"

"Well, for your sake, I hope they're good neighbors. 'Bye now. See you soon, I hope."

As Kendrik drove off, her face settled into an unaccustomed frown. Knock it off, old girl, she told herself sternly. You have neither the nerve nor the inclination to be a marriage buster—well, maybe a bit of the inclination.

Kendrik had put away the groceries and was peeling onions for a fish stew when she heard a car drive into the twisted, pin-straw-covered trail that led to the cottage. She was standing at the screen door, tears from the onion fumes running down her cheeks, when she was confronted by the very man she had spent so much time trying to put out of her mind. She thought of Vonnie's description as she took in his appearance in the sun-faded khaki-and-blue chambray. Brown hair just touched the collar of his shirt, and his curly sideburns showed a light frosting of gray.

"I thought you might be able to help me. Your friend Vonnie O'Neal said that you..." His voice trailed off as she looked up at him with tears swimming in her eyes.

"What is it?" he exclaimed. "Is something wrong?" Snatching open the screen door, he gathered her close before she could say a word.

Kendrik was momentarily stunned at the rush of feeling that overcame her at the touch of his warm, strong body. It was as if every cell in her body were suddenly put on standby alert. Then the ridiculous aspect of the situation struck her, and her shoulders began to shake with silent laughter.

"Let me go," she sputtered and struggled weakly, causing his arms to hold her even closer.

He stroked her hair. "There now, child, it's all right. Don't cry so."

Kendrik burst into peals of laughter, and Marcus released her so quickly she nearly stumbled. Helpless with laughter, she could only hold up the onion in one hand and the paring knife in the other.

"Oh, I see." His sheepish-sounding voice caused Kendrik to sober enough to look at him. An embarrassed expression covered his face, but his smile of abashment was completely disarming. "Well, it was nice as long as it lasted, regardless of the excuse."

The rest of the laughter left Kendrik's eyes as she surveyed this large, lean man who crowded the doorway and made dangerous riptides in her emotions.

"You said you needed help, Mr. Manning," she said, gesturing to the kitchen, bidding him enter. "I'll be glad to do what I can for you."

Marcus crossed to the chair she indicated and sat down as she settled herself again in the ladder-backed chair at the table.

"It's about the attic," he began. "The woman who took care of the place before I moved in, a Miss Tull, evidently didn't think of looking in the attic, and when I was up there yesterday checking for leaks, I saw an old box and a trunk." He pulled out a pipe and silently asked permission with a raised eyebrow.

Kendrik nodded, and he proceeded to fill it as he spoke. "I had no idea what to do with them. Miss Tull has moved to the mainland, and the real-estate agent was no help. Anyhow, I stopped in next door to thank the O'Neals for a jar of fig preserves they had left on the porch, and when I mentioned the things to them, they suggested I contact you. Why didn't you tell me it used to be your home?"

"Well, it wasn't exactly—that is, my parents moved to the mainland before I was born, but I used to visit my grandfather there every summer." She continued to slice potatoes and onions into the stoneware crock. In the moment of silence before she spoke again, Marcus was struck by a warmth of atmosphere surrounding this young woman and the small, homey cottage.

"Anyhow," she continued, "the house belongs to you now. To you and your wife. I'll get by as soon as I can and get the things out of your way."

Marcus stood up abruptly. "I don't have a wife," he said. "If you'll let me know when you're coming, I'll help you get the things into your car." He walked to the door as he spoke. "I'd better be getting on."

He was down the steps by the time Kendrik could reach the screen door. She called after him, "What about tomorrow? Will tomorrow afternoon be all right?"

"Fine. I'll be there."

Kendrik leaned against the doorframe and looked after the disappearing vehicle with unseeing eyes. I don't have a wife, I don't have a wife. Over and over the words repeated themselves in her head, only now beginning to sink into her consciousness.

Who was *Mrs.* Manning? She was sure the agent had said a Mr. and Mrs. Manning would be taking possession of the house in October. Mr. and Mrs. didn't sound like Mr. Manning and Mother. That would have been worded differently.

She walked slowly back to the kitchen, her mind busy with speculation as she automatically added the fish, the crisp cracklings, and the drippings to the vegetables in the pot. For that matter, who was Marcus Manning? she asked herself, idly shaking far too much salt and pepper into her stew. She covered the pot and shoved it into the oven, then sat down with an abstracted air.

After a while she took a deep breath. "Snap out of it, Ken, old girl!" she spoke aloud to herself.

Reaching for her banjo, she played for a long time, ignoring sore fingertips, unaware of whether she was playing badly or not.

CHAPTER FOUR

Kendrik was up early the next morning. The moonlight shining through the bedroom window and the mockingbird that sang all night long in the holly tree were not the only reasons she had trouble sleeping. Gulping down a glass of milk, she pulled a denim jacket on over last year's faded bikini. Opening the door of the little Bluebird for the eager Charlie, she drove them both to the beach.

It was late in the season for swimming, but it had been unseasonably warm up till now. Weather breeders, Grandy had called days like this. There was no one on the beach, and Kendrik threw off her jacket as she ran, Charlie yapping at her heels, and plunged into the breakers.

Wow! I must be crazy, she thought, as she came up shivering, but she quickly warmed up after diving under a few large waves and romping in the surf with the retriever. Just what I need to get rid of the tattered remnants of a sleepless night, she told herself, not attempting to escape the fact of her self-induced insomnia. Nighttime daydreams!

She whistled for the wet, sandy dog, and together they ran along the beach until Kendrik was gasping for breath and the old dog veered off to disinter a sand fiddler.

Gradually, her graceful lope across the wet sand slowed until she stopped, ankle deep in iridescent spume. She stood there in the opalescent early morning sunlight and watched the breakers roll in. They came in an orderly procession, expending their energy on the shore and quietly returning to the sea. Now and then a breaker much larger than the others would hit the beach with a riflelike report.

Kendrik rejoined the old dog waiting on the dunes, and together they returned to the car and drove back to the cottage. She felt exhausted and exhilarated at the same time.

Outside the cottage Kendrik played the hose over the sandy dog as well as her own feet and legs, then, impulsively, she aimed it at the salt-hazed windows. Admiring the glistening wetness of the glass, she walked slowly around the house, wetting down screens and windows and watching them dry again almost immediately to their previous salt-clouded condition. It would take a serious attack with cleanser and brush to undo the effect of several years of unattention.

Not today. The deleterious effects of a humid, salty atmosphere were taken for granted here on the outer banks, and Kendrik, admitting to herself the reason for her dawdling, had neither the time nor the interest to tackle the problem now.

Procrastination. That's all it was. Acknowledging that fact to herself, Kendrik went one step farther and recognized that had she not deliberately made herself go from one activity to another, she would have presented herself to Marcus at an indecently early hour.

After a quick shower, she sat on the porch and let the sunshine slowly dry her hair as her thoughts once more preceded her down to the other end of the island, to a certain house, a certain man.

What is the matter with me? You'd think I'd never seen a man before! He's nothing special, either. Not nearly as handsome as Scott. Old, too. Well, not really. Crochety, anyway. Bad temper, hateful sense of humor. She twisted a tendril of hair around a finger as she mused on her unexpected reaction to the man. Kendrik, my girl, you're looking for a father figure. But there was nothing daughterly about her reactions when he had held her close in the mistaken belief that she was crying.

The old brass Seth Thomas clock said almost five o'clock when Kendrik finally allowed herself to head for the village. As she drove along the narrow highway, doubts began to play on her mind. What if he had expected her much earlier? What if he had needed to go somewhere and had been held up on her account?

Irrationally, she regretted the combination of shyness and perversity that had held her back against all inclinations. By the time she pulled into the yard, she was almost overwhelmed by feelings of apprehension.

She knocked on the front door, her timidity diluted somewhat by the very strangeness of the action. This would be the first time she entered this house as a stranger, and had her host been anyone other than the man who so unaccountably engaged her imagination, she would have been saddened by feelings of loss.

Her mixed feelings underwent another change as she heard a muffled curse from somewhere inside, followed by the clatter of something heavy being dropped.

"Come in, damn it, come in! Ouch! Oh, hell!"

She opened the screen door and, following her instincts, hurried back to the kitchen. As she started to rush through the door at the sight of Marcus hunched over and holding both hands cupped before him, he barked out a command.

"Stop!" His voice was rough, and his eyes narrowed in his gray face. "There's grease all over the floor. Watch it!"

Kendrik paused long enough to take in the scene; the man, obviously in a great deal of pain, the heavy iron frying pan on the floor by the table, and the widening pool of smoking grease on the floor.

Carefully she stepped around the puddle and reached

over to turn off the red-hot burner. Then, turning to the man, she let her eyes drop to his hands. His left hand was glistening as the flesh reddened before her eyes. A grease burn. Excruciating! His other hand was drawn back so that she couldn't even see the hurt area.

Taking him by the arm, Kendrik quickly moved him to the sink, where she turned on the cold-water faucet. He plunged both hands in, sleeves and all, and the groan that escaped his pain-thinned lips made Kendrik cringe. Neither of them spoke for minutes. The water splashed into the sink and gurgled down the drain, and the clock on the sideboard ticked loudly. Those sounds only served to emphasize the pain-created silence.

After a while, a sigh touched her ears, and she felt her own tense muscles relax as the man beside her slowly straightened up. For the first time, he turned and looked directly at her.

"Sorry about this, girl."

"Oh, Marcus... Mr. Manning! Come on, let me drive you to the clinic," Kendrik insisted as she touched his arm gingerly and tried to move him toward the door.

Marcus stood firm. "No clinic. It's not serious, just hurt like blazes for a few minutes " He smiled a little grimly. "No pun intended."

"But burns are so dangerous—I mean, the possibility of infections—and the pain."

"Don't dither, child. If you want to be helpful, go look in the bathroom and find the tube of burn jelly and a roll of gauze. I think it's in the cabinet, but you may have to scramble around a bit."

Kendrik hurried into the old, familiar bathroom, noticing even in her haste the masculine aura of aftershave and some sort of woodsy smelling soap that had replaced the old liniment smell that once had permeated the room.

Hurrying back to the kitchen with her burden, she found Marcus seated at the table, both hands resting gingerly on their backs on the bare table top. He instructed her, and Kendrik spread the sterile jelly as gently as she could, flinching at every indication of his discomfort. Finally, the hands were swathed in clean white gauze, and Marcus leaned back in his chair and closed his eyes.

Kendrik cleared away the medical supplies and surveyed the mess.

"If you'll go into the living room and lie down, I'll clean up all this and make a pot of coffee. It won't take a minute."

"Honey, it's no way to treat a guest, but I'm going to let you do it. At the moment, I just don't feel like arguing."

He stood and, carefully avoiding the pool of grease, made his way from the kitchen. Kendrik looked after him anxiously, wondering if she should help him to bed instead, but he seemed steady enough on his feet and she had an idea he wouldn't welcome being fussed over. She tackled the task before her, first putting the kettle on to heat.

Later on, they were seated in the living room drinking coffee. His first cup had been liberally sweetened, at Kendrik's insistence, against shock. The second one was taken straight as Marcus explained what had happened.

"I was in my office. I suppose it was another bedroom when you knew it, but that's where I have my files, my desk, and so on. And I got involved trying to make heads and tails of a stack of bird-count reports for the past five years. I had turned on the fire under the kettle, I thought, but I'm not accustomed to the burner arrangement yet, and I switched on the wrong knob." He leaned back and closed his eyes momentarily, the pain he felt showing in the sharp-etched lines beside his mouth.

"Anyway," he continued after a moment, "I smelled something burning and went to investigate. The grease in the frying pan was smoking hot, in danger of bursting into flames, and like a damned fool I grabbed the handle with my bare hands! Not only that, as soon as I grabbed it, I dropped it and sloshed hot fat all over the other hand." He shook his head slowly in disgust. "No excuse. Just plain stupidity! My head was still back in the office, I suppose, trying to decipher field notes." His eyes suddenly widened, and with a half-stifled curse, he quickly stood up and left the room.

Kendrik sat where she was for a moment, curious, hesitant, and not a little alarmed. Then, moving swiftly once she made up her mind, she followed him into the hall.

Marcus was leaning in the doorway of a room that had once been a combination sewing, ironing, and storage room. She stopped, blocked by his large, well-knit figure, and peered past him into chaos.

"I just remembered that in my haste to get up from that bad excuse for a table, I knocked against the corner and collapsed a leg, or something. The table's . . . not mine," he explained in a rather grim tone. Stepping into the room, he reached out a bandaged hand to right the drunken-looking little card table, wincing as he made contact.

"Let me," suggested Kendrik, and she moved past him and reached up under the offending table and, after a short struggle locked the leg into place. Rising, she turned her attention to the mass of papers scattered across the floor. Marcus made only perfunctory protests as she began to try to stack up the miscellaneous pages. There were official-looking forms, onion-skin pages covered with smudged carbon, pages torn from notebooks with Latin-looking words and long strings of figures, even envelopes with notes scribbled across the back.

"I'm afraid I'm not the best-organized person in the world," he apologized.

"The best? You're not even the worst! You're not organized to any degree at all!" Kendrik retorted, amusement and amazement in her voice.

After a while the light was switched on against the gathering gloom, and under Marcus's direction, Kendrik was able to make a start at sorting the piles of papers. She would probably have continued longer had she not looked up and seen the grayness returning to his usually bronzed face.

"Oh, you should be resting," she exclaimed. "Not only that, but you haven't had any dinner!" Suddenly aware of her own emptiness, she stood up, placing a steadying hand on the pile of papers they had already sorted.

"Look, I don't know what you had planned for tonight, but if you'll let me—I mean—" She broke off, self-conscious again under the steady appraisal of his brilliant eyes.

"We could go out to eat. I certainly owe you a dinner, but I'm not too sure I could handle myself too well with these." He grinned ruefully, holding up his gauze mitts.

"Let me take a look in the pantry, if you've stocked up, or I could go—"

"If you don't mind too much, I think you'll find a can of something you could heat for us."

Kendrik enjoyed the simple meal of soup, salad, and cheese toast more than any she had had in a long time. The enforced relaxation and intimacy made her eyes sparkle even more than was usual. She would have loved to prolong the occasion, but her better judgment made her stand and gather her handbag and keys soon after the dishes were cleared away.

She had brought Marcus some aspirin to take, for his hands were obviously causing him a good deal of pain.

"If you'd like"—she made the offer hesitantly—"I can come back in the morning and make breakfast for you. Then I can finish sorting your notes."

"I can manage with cold cereal. But, if it's not asking too much, I could use help with the papers. Just for an hour or so."

"Oh, I'll be glad to help for as long as it takes. I'm really sort of coasting these days. Vacationing before looking for work. I—I'd like to help."

"I suppose I could ask the O'Neals. Vonnie is some sort of nurse, I understand."

Kendrik's heart plunged as he spoke, but he continued, "However, come to think of it, when I spoke to them for a few minutes this morning, they were just leaving for Norfolk. Vonnie's taking her mother to the doctor for her regular treatment, and she said it will be several days before they get back."

"Oh," Kendrik commented, feeling unaccountably young and rather awkward as she stood there, wanting to make the most of this excuse for further contact.

"I'm taking advantage of your good nature, but unless I'm to get hopelessly behind in my working schedule, I have little choice. That is, if you're honestly willing."

"Oh, I am, I am." She laughed in relief. "See you in the morning."

CHAPTER FIVE

So began a time of exquisite pleasure for Kendrik. She would have liked to prepare three meals a day for him, but Marcus insisted on maintaining as much independence as possible. She made sandwiches at noon and several pots of coffee during the day, but most of the time was spent in the room he called his office. She found she was torn between wanting to be admirably efficient for this man and wanting to prolong the job as long as possible.

The feeling of being in this old, familiar place with this new, exciting man was strange. Often Kendrik's fingers would slow to a halt on the typewriter keyboard as her eyes settled on the man seated by the window, awkwardly shuffling through more notes for her to copy. It was not so much a case of her thinking of him constantly, more that he was fast becoming a part of her consciousness. Like her arm, or her leg. Not thought about, just always within awareness.

On more than one occasion she felt his eyes on her as she bent over the notes she was copying. At such times she found herself blushing and making idiotic mistakes. He must have thought her a terrible typist, for all too often as she felt his eyes upon her, her fingers would fumble and she would have to pull up the sheet and make erasures.

It was natural for Kendrik to reminisce about her life as a child in this house. Small things would occur or words be spoken that would prompt certain recollections, and she would find herself relating the story of why the kitchen cabinets were all hung upside down, or how a particular scar came to be in the woodwork. She told him some of the stories she had made up about the rather ambiguous figure in the stained-glass window set

29

unexpectedly in the wall at one end of the kitchen.

Marcus, for his part, was unnaturally silent on these occasions. He listened with complete absorption, often smiling in advance of the end of the story, as though he somehow anticipated the outcome. Kendrik, at home in these familiar surroundings and basking in the warmth of the situation, was far too immersed in her own happiness to see him objectively.

Now that he didn't talk. He did. But always about the work they were doing. About the activities of various wildlife groups, or the odd habits of certain shorebirds. He shared openly with her several interesting happenings in the field, but as far as his personal life was concerned, he was more than reticent. She knew nothing at all about him, only that she longed for each night to end so that she could turn the little gray Bluebird southwest and hurry to join him each morning.

As his hands improved, Marcus was able to do more and more, and it was obvious that she would not be needed much longer. Kendrik felt the loss already, for soon there would be no excuse at all to see this man, and he had indicated no personal interest in her at all. On the rare occasions when she accidentally touched him, he seemed to withdraw into himself even more.

Puzzled, but inherently friendly, rather like a puppy who can't understand why its overtures are not welcomed by all, Kendrik made a last attempt to prolong her stay on a particular Thursday when all possible work she could do was finished.

"Do you know, we never did get the box and trunk from the attic," she reminded Marcus as they stood in the hallway.

"No, I guess we were sidetracked," he admitted smilingly. "Well, come along. No time like the present."

He led her toward the narrow, steep stairway at the back of the house.

"Grandy always planned to put a light here, but he never got around to it. We seldom used them, anyway. The stairs, not lights." She grinned.

Marcus gestured for her to precede him and put out a hand to steady her as she neared the top. She hoped he hadn't noticed her reaction to his touch, but as he held the door open for her to pass through, he was careful not to touch her again.

They stood for a moment in the large, almost empty space, and both were caught up in the atmosphere of warmth, almost mesmerized by the shaft of late-afternoon sunshine that captured the fall of a few dust motes on the way to the aged wooden floor. The single overhead bulb did little to disperse the benevolent gloom, the almost palpable presence of faded, gentle memories, like flowers pressed in a book.

Kendrik felt her mind drawn back to rainy days of childhood spent playing with paper dolls up here in her own world. There had been many other boxes then, an old quilting frame, and a dress form that became a huge doll. She remembered the button box as she walked over to a corner of the room where an errant ray of sunshine had picked out a tiny rhinestone embedded in a black button.

As she picked it up, she turned to see Marcus watching her, perhaps seeing in his mind's eye a thin, small girl sitting on the floor playing with paper dolls cut from the mail-order catalog. The odd expression in his eyes was gone in a second, and Kendrik felt a loss as the familiar shutters closed over his shadowed blue eyes.

She spoke quickly to dispel the tangible silence. "If you'll help me drag this trunk over to the stairs, maybe we can slide it down."

"It's not heavy. I think I can manage if you'll get the door for me." He lifted the old humpbacked trunk to his shoulder and carried it down to the foot of the stairs as Kendrik bent over the cardboard box. Unfolding the flaps, she lifted off several sheets of yellowed, crumbling newspaper. The odor of mothballs assailed her nostrils as she unfolded a musty old quilt, its colors still gleaming as richly as a stained-glass window. The random pattern of its patches was emphasized by the fernlike tracery of embroidery. Kendrik felt her eyes begin to brim as she looked up at the man who had silently rejoined her.

"I remember this." Her voice was almost a whisper. "My grandmama gave it to Mother, and when Mother died, it somehow didn't seem right to take it to the apartment. Grandy said it would be here waiting for me whenever I wanted it. I was fifteen then."

She was once again that rather gawky child, distraught at the loss of her mother, unable to speak of that loss to the grim, silent man her father had become almost overnight.

Marcus brought her back to the present, speaking quietly. "I suppose my mother had a quilt, too. I wouldn't know. She and Father and all they owned were washed away in a flash flood when a dam burst close to where we lived. I was away at boarding school then. I just stayed. There was nothing to come home for, no home to come to." He seemed suddenly embarrassed at this personal revelation.

Instinctively Kendrik reached out a sympathetic hand to Marcus, and as she touched his arm, he turned to her, and almost without thought, his arms went around her. She rested her head on his chest, and they were, in a way, each consoling two inconsolable children.

They stood thus for countless moments, neither of

them moving, neither of them speaking. Then, as Kendrik became aware of the beat of his heart under her cheek, she raised her face, her eyes seeking something—understanding?—in his.

The thing that flared between them had nothing at all to do with a fifteen-year-old girl or a young boarding-school student. It was as if they were compelled by a powerful magnet, and she was trembling almost uncontrollably by the time his mouth touched hers. She responded to his kiss with all the ardor of her generous young heart, and as his lips demanded, then beseeched her own, she became aware of the thunder of their combined heartbeat resounding in the dry, silent old room.

Suddenly, inexplicably, he thrust her from him, turning his back and clenching his fists at his sides.

"Marcus," she whispered, "what's wrong?"

"Go, will you?" he snarled. "Just get out of here for now."

He turned and, as she would have spoken, held up a restraining hand.

"Kendrik . . . sweet child, little girl . . . please just go," he said, attempting a smile and failing miserably.

She fled, not stopping even as she heard his voice call after her.

CHAPTER SIX

There's something about the quality of light in the fall of the year that's peculiarly evocative. The angle of the sun speaks silently of seasons past and time to come, but declares a sort of moratorium of its own.

Into the hushed, dazzling clarity of late October, Kendrik moved as one in a dream. She stood by the single section of picket fence, which was covered by some sturdy rose bushes, with scissors in her hand and an abstracted look on her face, her head slightly tilted on the long, delicate neck.

Let's see, she mused to herself, there must be a reason for me being here by the lovely, frosted blue-green of this old vine . . . mildew! Oh, yes. It had been on her mind ever since she arrived to try to come to terms with the rambler, but looking at it now, its powdery leaves reminding her of the Dusty Miller that straggled through the abandoned flower beds in front of the porch, she hadn't the drive to tackle the long-neglected job.

She sat down on the pine-straw-covered ground, leaning up against the rough bark of an old pine tree, and felt the sun's warmth sinking into her bones. Though she was not unhappy, she carefully avoided letting her mind touch on certain subjects. Only by drifting in a sort of limbo could she avoid the searing memory of Marcus—of his flame blue eyes penetrating her soul, leaving her more vulnerable than she had ever been.

Even a visit from Vonnie, her gray-green eyes snapping as she poured forth her usual chatter, did little to lift Kendrik from the lethargy into which she had sunk.

"Her-High-and-Mightiness came home last night," Vonnie announced in a mincing little voice.

"Erma? Hmmmm. You'll enjoy that."

"Not for long, I won't," came the sharp reply. "She took over my room because the other one is 'too small,' and her clothes are bulging out of everything in the house! I'd suspect my sister was moving back for good if I didn't know her. About three days among the peasants is all Erma can take. All the peasants can take, too!" She giggled.

"Ummm-hmmm."

"What's happened to you, Kendrik? Are you sick or something? I might as well be talking to the clothesline pole for all the response I get!" Vonnie stood up to go. "You'd better be figuring out what's wrong with you and getting squared away, because there's a storm making up off Miami and it'll probably be a hurricane by tonight."

After Vonnie left, Kendrik stood, leaning against the satiny weathered fence. What was wrong with her? Was she coming down with something? A suspicion that had been floating just below the level of consciousness for several days began to drift up to the surface. Oh, no, she thought. You don't fall in love just like that! Not with one kiss, some angry words, and a few impersonal hours spent working together! I don't even know the man. I don't know anything about him! Kendrik Haynes, you will not do this foolish thing! Kendrik Haynes, her mind whispered back, you have done this foolish thing.

Having once admitted to herself the true state of affairs, she relaxed and almost reveled in reliving those precious few moments spent with Marcus in the attic. One part of her mind stood back, knowing the pain would come soon enough, but for now it was enough just to speak his name aloud as she sat on the dunes looking out over a strangely restless sea. She would smile, then, catching herself smiling, would laugh.

It was like the return of someone dear from a long journey. In the beginning it was enough just to know he was back, to experience the joy. Later would come the time of questions, the where, why, when, and what.

End of analogy. For later still would come the pain. A part of her that ran beneath the level of mind—a part that had to do with emotions, with intuition—knew there would be pain.

Marcus was an experienced man, a very desirable man, and Kendrik was aware of her own limitations. She considered her looks. Hair, light brown—not platinum blonde but just ordinary dried grass color. Eyes, green—not violet or amber or anything exotic—just sort of sea green. She wasn't tall and willowy or tiny and delicate, but just average. Her waist looked so small only because her hips swelled in what Grandy had reassured her was a womanly way, and both her neck and her legs were a trifle too long.

Not only that, she had never gone anywhere or done anything exciting. Summers, while her friends hiked all over Europe or sailed across the Gulf of Mexico, she came here to this small, desolate stretch of sand where most of the people lived and died without ever going more than fifty miles away. There were no fine mansions here, and if some people had more material advantages than others, it was seldom discernible. As old Miss Tull had said once when Kendrik was visiting, "You can only sleep in one bed at a time, and rich or poor, we all live on collards and croakers down here."

Thinking of the old woman who had been so much a part of Kendrik's summers reminded her again of the trunk and the box in Marcus's attic. She had come away without them. Her mother's quilt was probably still on the floor where she had dropped it.

Hugging close her newfound feelings for Marcus, Kendrik knew she could not face him without a certain amount of embarrassment. There had been no hiding the fact from him that she was completely under the spell of his kiss that day when pity had touched off such a flame. He must think her a silly, susceptible schoolgirl. Even so, it was time to get off dead center. She desperately wanted to see him again, in light of her newly discovered love, much in the way one probes a painful tooth.

First thing in the morning! Yes, a cool, businesslike approach in the early morning would be the least apt to be awkward. After all, moonlight and roses romances weren't as potent in the bright, clear light of day, with the smell of bacon frying and the sound of outboard motors creating a cheerful, no-nonsense atmosphere.

She slept better that night than she had for some time, and it was almost nine-thirty before she awoke.

Sometime during the night, a light, determined sort of rain had commenced, and it looked as if it meant to settle down for a long stay.

With no radio or television, Kendrik had not been reminded of Vonnie's words about a hurricane, and all thoughts of the weather had been relegated to the back of her mind. Now, reminded by the rain, she saw again the puffy little cottonballs scurrying along the horizon yesterday. There had been sort of an uncanny quietness, and come to think of it, the usual cacophony of seagulls had been missing.

"Oh, no!" she said. Grabbing her usual garb of jeans and jersey, she dressed with haste, not bothering to put on shoes, and coaxing up a reluctant engine, drove swiftly toward the village. If a hurricane was really on the way, she would need extra supplies. The small, wooded point of land where the cottage was located was separated from the village by almost three miles of low, flat beachland, and high tides or heavy rains could make it impassable to all but four-wheel-drive vehicles.

As she passed through the white and unpainted shingled houses huddling down in the dark growths of yaupon and live oak, she glanced in the direction of the weather bureau. High on the flag pole above the observation room were two black-centered red squares. Hurricane signals.

She hurried on by, wondering, not for the first time, whether to bother with the trunk today. It was silly in this weather to even consider it, but childish as it was, Kendrik knew she could not resist an opportunity to see Marcus again.

She stopped the car as close to the house as possible. Running for the shelter of the front porch, she didn't stop to wonder if he was home. She knocked on the white-paneled door, called out, and was reaching to knock again when the door was opened by a beautiful woman with hair the color of polished copper.

"Erma! What are you... I mean, I thought—" She stopped, at a loss for words.

"Oh, it's the Haynes girl, isn't it?" Erma didn't open the screen door but stood perfectly still in a clingy jumpsuit of an improbable shade of pink. It should have looked awful on a redhead, but it didn't. Erma O'Neal knew her style. "Did you want something?"

"Mr. Manning... is he here? There was a trunk, a box, and he said..." She stammered to a halt. For some reason, Erma had always had that effect on her. Under the circumstances, it was doubled in spades.

Erma looked over her shoulder, then back at the damp girl on the porch. Her ripe-olive eyes shone opaquely, like dark glass that baffled all attempts to penetrate. "I'm sure it's nothing that can't wait. Naturally, Marcus and I have too much to do now to bother about an old trunk. We'll see that you get it later. Now, if you don't mind..."

Looking at the blankness of the closed door, Kendrik was stunned. Erma? Erma O'Neal and Marcus?

Even the flush that covered her lowered face could not counteract the chill that seeped into her heart as she made her way blindly through the rain.

As she switched on the engine, her movements those of an automation, she thought she heard a voice call her name, but she drove off.

She was halfway home before she remembered the supplies. Reversing and turning around on the empty road, she sighed to herself. Well, you silly calf, unless you plan to pine away within the next few days, you'll have to have groceries!

When she finally left the little general store, its lights gleaming yellow through the steamy windows, she turned the loaded car north and proceeded slowly through the driving rain.

She saw no one as she passed through the village, most people having long since heard news of the storm and battened down. She felt a perfect fool to have ignored all the obvious signs—the cracking breakers hitting the shore a few days ago, the oily restlessness of the water yesterday, the vacuumlike stillness, and the absence of birds.

Backing the car up as close to the porch as possible, she began unloading boxes, the melting, wet cardboard spilling cans and jars along the way.

Charlie whickered softly from under the porch, his light brown eyes pleading with her for a word of comfort.

"It's all right, boy. You'll be high and dry up under there. I'll give you a hambone to keep your mind off your troubles."

Kendrik had long since accepted the fact that Charlie was not a house dog. Teeth marks on chair rungs and claw marks on door facings attested to the fact that Charlie could not relax unless he was free to roam when the spirit moved him.

Already drenched to the skin, she decided to tackle the outside chores before the wind picked up any more. She left the pile of damp provender in the middle of the floor and returned to the rainy gloom. With the aid of a ladder and a hammer, she managed to secure the storm blinds. She gathered up anything that might blow away—a bucket, a pair of rubber boots. Let's see, what else? Water. In the shed were two juniper barrels that would do to collect rainwater in. If the power went off, as it probably would, the electric water pump would be useless. The fragrance of the white cedar, locally called juniper, made her think of the traditional fishing boats along that section of the coast. Juniper was long-lasting and lightweight and was the favorite boat-building material, but even sweeter memories were of drinking water from juniper barrels when she was small, a custom that had passed since the coming of plastic coolers.

Barrels rolled into position, she went inside, and though the power was still on, she lighted an oil lamp, liking the friendly, warm glow and the subtle odor.

She peeled off her wet clothes and ran a hot tub. It would probably be the last time for a few days that she could count on hot water, if the power failed. Sinking down into the fragrant bath, she thought of other storms she had experienced, feeling again the exhilaration of rushing to prepare, everybody with certain responsibilities, of sitting around during the full force of the storm listening to the older members of the family talk about hurricanes of other days, always bigger, always wilder.

She pictured Grandy stepping up to the barometer on the kitchen wall every few minutes, tapping and reporting, "Still fallin'." Mother would wring out the towels, placed on the windowsill to soak up the rain that beat in in spite of all they could do, and she herself would check the attic, running from bucket to pot to pan, all collecting water from the leaky roof, to see which needed emptying.

"We built our homes right where the Indians had their villages two, three hundred years ago," Grandy would say. "They knew how to survive."

The difference, Kendrik thought as she stepped out of the rapidly cooling water, is that now I'm alone. She felt safe enough, but as it grew darker outside and the wind began to shriek louder still, she drew herself up into a small, flannel-covered ball on the sofa and piped bravely on her recorder to try to drown out the furies howling to get in.

Much later, drinking her third cup of coffee, she found her mind turning again to Marcus. Like touching a bruise to see if it still hurt, she thought of Erma, so much at home there. Neighborliness was one thing, but Erma had seemed *so* at home there, so possessive. Erma was of his world, a world that someone as gauche and inexperienced as Kendrik could never hope to attain. Oh, for the poise, the sophistication, and the beauty of Erma, for the looks that could captivate and the mind that could intrigue!

"Oh, damn." Kendrik sighed and, getting up, she paced restlessly to the door. She opened it slightly and looked outside, noting the faintest glimmer of moonlight. The rain had almost stopped, and the wind had suddenly dropped to nothing. She opened the door wider and stood there in the doorway, looking out into the moon-shadowed yard.

Under the porch, Charlie whimpered softly.

"I hear you, old fellow," she called softly. "It's not over yet, so settle down."

The stillness of the moment was uncanny, broken only by an occasional splash of water dripping from the gutter into the rainbarrel, and by a light.

A light? Kendrik peered through the screen door at the wavering, flickering light coming from the direction of the main road. Not a car. She would have heard it. Besides, the road was probably awash, and it would get even deeper after the brief respite of the hurricane eye passed and the tail end of the storm whipped the sound up out of its banks.

The light turned into the path leading to the cottage, and Kendrik stepped out on the porch, wondering who would be coming in this weather at this time of night to check on her. Surely the islanders would know she was secure on high ground with the cutting edge of the wind dulled by the woods around her.

As the tall, yellow-slickered figure approached the house, a void suddenly opened up somewhere under her ribcage. Marcus!

Forgotten was the sight of Erma in her provocative jumpsuit lounging so possessively in his doorway. Forgotten were their angry words, her embarrassment, his puzzling abruptness. Remembered only was that this was the man she loved. He had somehow managed to cover the three miles that separated them during the wild darkness of wind-lashed rain.

"Are you all right?" Anxiety put a rough edge to his words. "Kendrik!" He jumped up the last two steps and stood dripping before her, massive in his yellow oilskins and sou'wester. Wet rubber boots glistened in the light from the room beyond.

"Marcus, how did you...you shouldn't have..." She

stumbled over her words, wanting only to throw her arms about the wet, dripping man before her. "Here, come inside. Don't worry about dripping, you can leave your wet things out here in the front room." She closed the door behind him.

Hanging his rain gear on a peg on the wall, he turned to look at her. His face had lost its tan, and there was a grayness emphasizing lines she hadn't seen before. His eyes were dark with concern. "Mr. Rustino at the store told me you were still here. It never occurred to me that you'd stay here alone! When you came to the house this morning I was upstairs putting buckets under the roof leaks, and before I could get down again you were gone. Why didn't you wait?" His strong hand came out to grasp her upper arm, and his eyes sought hers inquiringly. "Kendrik? Erma said you had stopped by to say hello and were in too great a rush to stay."

"Would you like a cup of coffee?" Kendrik offered. Erma! She remembered all the times she had been crushed by one of Erma's trenchant observations. A new haircut had suddenly seemed a disaster when Erma raised an eyebrow and asked what on earth had happened to her head. A favorite dress became a rag when laughingly remarked on the sheer guts it took to wear a rig like that. Well, Erma was back again, and Kendrik would shrivel up and die before she would subject herself to the comments her feelings for Marcus would bring forth!

Busying herself in the tiny kitchen, she resolved to put an end to her love—surely just an infatuation. Whatever feelings she had for Marcus may as well die a-borning for all the good they would do her.

As she handed him the mug of black coffee and indicated a chair, she tried to think of an innocuous subject to discuss. The obvious one was the weather, of course. She opened her mouth to ask how deep the water on the road was and heard, to her chagrin, her own treacherous voice asking how long he had known Erma.

"Oh, several years. I met her when she was doing television interviews. Why?"

"N-nothing." She felt a red tide rise to her face. "I mean, no reason. I just wondered. She—she's very beautiful, isn't she?"

"Yes, she is. She's a good sport, too."

"I suppose you saw a lot of her," Kendrik suggested, horrified at herself but unable to keep from probing the relationship.

"I suppose I did," Marcus replied, lifting one eyebrow as if to question her interest in his personal life.

Kendrik's eyes wandered around the room, unable to meet his own cool amusement. She studied with great interest the knot in the paneling beside her chair until the silence made her acutely uncomfortable.

"Well, after all, I suppose you two have a lot in common, don't you? I mean, friends and—and all." She tapered off as he stood abruptly and walked over to the door.

"Kendrik, you're a sweet girl and a bit too good-looking for my peace of mind. And though I'm a few years older than you, that doesn't mean I'm not susceptible to physical attraction." He turned suddenly and leveled a hard look at her as she cowered in her chair, acutely conscious of the well-worn, faded flannel nightgown and her touseled hair and naked face. "The kiss that happened between us in my attic was just a physical reaction to too much time spent in close company. If you nurtured any schoolgirlish ideas, forget them!"

She gasped. "Oh! You're unbelievable! I don't believe any man can be as conceited and obnoxious as you are!

Did you think for one moment I was interested in you? Don't be silly! I'm—practically engaged to a man I knew at school—S-Scott Chandler—and anyway—" Her eyes brimmed over with rage, humiliation, and...something else.

Marcus sighed and reached out a hand as if to touch her hair, but she jerked away with a sob.

"Look, girl, I didn't mean to embarrass you, but I thought it only fair to level with you. I owe you a lot for all the help you gave me, and I'd like to be friends. Your grandfather and I knew each other for years, and he used to talk about you when I visited him during drum seasons. He was proud of you, you know. He told me a long time ago he intended to give you this cottage when he no longer needed the rent money from it."

All of a sudden, something clicked in place, and Kendrik heard again her grandfather telling her about his friend who wrote for sports magazines and did a series of television programs on migratory wildfowl.

"You're Mark Marksman! Grandy used to talk about you for hours! But I thought you were an—an—"

"An older man? That's just it, Kendrik, I *am* an older man. I'm thirty-two, and I've been around more than I care to admit. The women I've known, including the one I almost married, knew the score. I didn't leave behind me a trail of tender, bleeding hearts because I carefully avoided tender hearts in the first place!" He seemed to grow colder and angrier before her eyes, and Kendrik shivered.

Outside, a branch tapped against the wall, heralding the return of the winds from another quarter. Marcus moved restlessly about the room, touching the books, the instrument cases, looking everywhere but at the girl in the big, shabby old lounge chair.

"You don't have to worry about me," she began. "I

certainly wouldn't be interested in a—a man your age. And anyway, I'm not at all impressed by so-called physical attractions. There are much more important things to consider in a—a man—woman relationship."

Marcus directed a look of amused contempt her way, and she felt the warmth rising in her face. Despite her embarrassment, she stubbornly continued to look directly into those cool, blue eyes, and she saw the coolness give way to a smile. At least, his eyes narrowed and glinted as his firm, wide mouth lifted on one side.

"Full marks for spunk, honey. You'll be a hell of a woman when you grow up."

"Grow up!" she exploded. "I'm twenty-two!"

"And fresh out of school. And when you weren't in school you were at home with Mama and Papa or here with Grandpapa. Kendrik, I've seen girls in high school who have been around more than you have. Girls who could hold their own with men of any age. You're different, and it's a nice difference. One of these days you'll meet some fine young man—your friend Scott maybe—and marry and settle down with a family and two cars, one dog, and a mortgage. He'll be a lucky fellow."

Kendrik dangled a felt slipper on the toe of one bare foot and watched it intently as she inquired, "What about you? You said you almost got married. What happened?"

"Remember the day we first met? If you can call it that." He grinned and took out a cigarette. "I was mad as hell because my charming financee had dumped me two days before the ceremony. It was the finest thing she ever did for me, but at the time it hurt like hell—pride, I guess."

"Didn't you love her? Surely more was involved than pride?"

"Love Sheila? No, I don't think love entered into it for either one of us. I'm afraid I'll have to disillusion you, child, but few, if any, marriages are based on love. Some work out well enough—as long as both parties stick to the agreement. My parents fought every day till they were killed. I don't suppose either one of them was at fault. I guess they were basically fine people. But they both wanted different things. Dad was a rover. He had itchy feet and couldn't understand why Mom wasn't willing to live out of a suitcase with him. What she wanted the most in the world was a home. She was a natural nest builder. The worst of all was having me. I was the prime mistake." He laughed bitterly, and Kendrik was reminded of the surge of feeling that had triggered that kiss in the attic weeks ago.

"At any rate, I learned from them. I learned to enjoy women where I found them and move on when things threatened to get sticky. That way, nobody was ever hurt."

"But what about Sheila?"

"Oh, yes. Well, I gurss we all have our vulnerable moments. About the same time I got the assignment to write, or rather to rewrite a series of articles on migratory wildfowl for publication as a book, Sheila decided she'd like to marry. I needed a house near Pea Island Refuge, your grandfather's place came on the market, Sheila convinced me I'd need a woman to help take care of it, and before I woke up, I was almost tied. It was a lucky thing for both of us that she had another fish on the line at the same time, not that I knew anything about it then. He not only had more money, but was willing to spend it in more exciting places, and it didn't take but a phone call to switch over to a more promising prospect."

"But that's awful! She couldn't have dropped you like that if she had really—"

"Loved me? I told you, love didn't enter into it. When I

met Sheila, I was doing a lot of television work and running with a pretty fast crowd. It was her idea of glamour, I guess, although as far as I was concerned, the tinsel was pretty tarnished. I was ready to settle down to birdwatching and writing with maybe an occasional fishing trip to Acapulco or Bimini. Anyhow, since the house was already bought and the contract for the book signed, I came on down here. I'm such a methodical old drybones, I hate having my plans disrupted at the last moment, I guess, and I was still close to the boiling point when I ran afoul of your dog on the beach that day."

"Where does Erma come in?" Kendrik asked, determined to clear up all her unanswered questions while the storm had them closed up together.

"It was through Erma that I met Sheila. They were close friends. Still are, I guess. Erma and I knew each other from TV days, and we've both worked for the same publisher for a couple of years. She's a good sport. No stickiness involved—she plays by my rules." He gave her a meaningful look and then moved over to the door. "The rain's stopped. I expect the worst is over."

Kendrik came and stood beside him, and while her head was busy filing away all the excellent reasons for forgetting all about this man, her heart betrayed her completely when he dropped a casual arm about her shoulder. She held her breath for a long moment, and as she expelled it in a long, quivering sigh, conscious in every cell of her body of his nearness, he looked down at her.

"What's the matter, Kendrik? Cold?"

She shook her head, unwilling to look up at him. "You don't need to baby-sit with me anymore, Marcus. I can take care of myself."

"Can you? I wonder." With a deft movement he turned her to him and looked down at her flushed face. "Damn," he said softly. "Didn't you hear a word I said?" He moved one hand up over her shoulder, under her hair to the warm, vulnerable nape. His fingers on her sensitive skin sent tremors through her body, and unable to help herself, she lifted her face to kiss his.

Moments later, moments in which her susceptibility was cruelly revealed, he released her abruptly. Kendrik reached behind her to brace herself on the wall, feeling the terrible loss of his strength and his warmth. It took enormous effort on her part to raise her chin and speak in a voice that scarcely trembled at all.

"Th-that was not necessary! I told you I—I don't need anything from you. I can take care of myself!"

Marcus removed his rain gear from the peg and opened the door. He stood in the opening for a long moment, shoulders hunched, head slightly down. Then he turned and burned a direct look into her eyes. "Take care of yourself, can you? What does it take to show you, you little fool? You're vulnerable to any experienced man who comes along!" Quickly he stepped outside, closing the screen door between them. "I pity the next poor fellow who comes along. He's apt to end up securely tied before he knows what hit him. Lucky for me I was immunized, wasn't it?" His laugh was not a pleasant one as he loped down the steps and disappeared into the dripping pine shadows.

A few minutes ago, Kendrik thought, you were telling me what a lucky fellow my husband would be. Could it be that the great Marcus Manning was a wee bit rattled?

CHAPTER SEVEN

During the week after the hurricane, Kendrik, like most of the other islanders, spend a good bit of time in beachcombing, surveying the changes the storm had brought about, and making minor repairs. There were always a few losses, but none to compare with those on other stretches of the banks where the tourist trade had fostered an overgrowth of beach houses, motels, and junk joints. The forces of nature seemed almost to respect the sturdy, unpretentious wooden houses and usually passed over them with a minimum of damage. Homes, boats, and outbuildings that had been built by the capable island men could usually be repaired by those same men.

Charlie was a familiar sight pursuing dispossessed muskrats across the beach, as were barefooted children in shorts and heavy sweaters picking excitedly through the odd assortment of jetsam.

Kendrik wandered along the shore frequently, feeling almost insulated against thought. Her music was a thing of the past, for too many of the old ballads were sad songs of lost love. She dug out her fishing tackle and tried her luck in the early mornings and again late in the evenings, depending on the tide. After catching enough to satisfy her diminished appetite, however, there seemed little reason to continue fishing.

Of Marcus she saw nothing. It was almost as if he had ceased to exist,except for the steady ache that was a constant companion, remaining just out of reach, like a dream of pain.

Her healthy young spirit, in an effort to overcome the apathy into which she had lapsed, began to crave the company of other young people. A party of some sort, an excuse to get together with a large group and block out this solitary yearning for one man—yes, that would do it!

Vonnie would be a big help in rounding up enough for a lively gathering, and when, on the same morning the idea had occurred to her, she ran into the dark-haired young nurse in the post office, what had been only a tentative plan took off like a rocket.

Kendrik had consciously avoided the O'Neal home for fear of encountering Erma. Somehow, she was not ready for that yet. Nor did she inquire about her, but as names were added to the party list, Vonnie volunteered the information that Erma had returned to her job.

"Our new neighbor, Mr. Manning—oh-o-o! You've seen him, haven't you? Tall, tan, and terrific!" Vonnie rolled her expressive eyes. "It seems he and Erma were quite an item for a while, and I'm pretty sure now that that's why she came home. She heard he was moving down here and didn't let any grass grow under her feet before she trailed him down."

Kendrik was torn between a burning need to hear his name spoken aloud and a desire to appear uninterested.

"Well, I don't think there'll be any wedding bells," Vonnie said. "He's too wary a fish to get caught with that bait! She positively drips all over him like a melted candle, though, and he doesn't seem to mind too much—in fact, they left together. When he mentioned having to go to Norfolk to see his editor, she suddenly developed this burning passion to get back to her job! Ha!" Vonnie tucked a wispy curl behind her ear, picked up her ballpoint, and began to write again.

"Let's see, there's Buck, or course, and Jeff, his older brother. Remember him? He's home for a while now. He's the only one of those Hollis boys who doesn't have anything to do with boats. We can ask him, and I'll get the

Marvin girls to ask those boys from the weather bureau. Leave it to me! I'll have plenty of people there!"

Kendrik's face began to regain some of its former sparkle. "If we have it out on the beach, we can go out early and get clams, fish, and maybe some crabs. There'll be plenty of food then, no matter how many come. The boys can bring the beer, and I'll do some baking, and oh, yes, there's a huge old coffeepot in the shed. I'll bring it, too. Now, what else?"

The two girls, so different in appearance, huddled together for several minutes, making plans, then went their separate ways. As Kendrik left the tiny post office she seemed more like the open, carefree girl who had crossed the ferry to her island home such a short time ago. Strong inner resources came to her aid in healing the grievous wound she had so recently received. She carefully avoided touching scars.

The idea of a beach party was taken up with enthusiasm by the young people of the island, for entertainment was limited, and as winter bore down on them, it seemed a good opportunity to gather one more time. Willing hands took over the arrangements for food and drink, and Kendrik, going about more freely now that there was no danger of seeing either Marcus or Erma, was received eagerly and greeted on all sides with excitement.

"Looks like it's going to be a full-moon party, Ken."

"Bring your instruments! There'll be plenty more, and we'll have a real hoedown!"

"What if the fish don't bite? Are we all invited to your cottage for supper?"

"They'll bite, they'll bite!" Kendrik called back, loading her old sedan with an assortment of baking ingredients that had almost strained the resources of the old-fashioned general store.

The weather held up beautifully, remaining unseasonably warm during the days and cooling to an autumn chill after darkness had fallen. Perfect for an afternoon spent gathering seafood and an evening spent cooking, eating, and making music around a campfire.

At about the same time Kendrik was pulling on her blue jeans and her black, turtleneck sweater in preparation for the party, the squatty five-car ferry that served the island was preparing to leave the mainland with its two cars and three passengers. Sitting alone beside the driver's seat of the four-wheel-drive sports wagon was a smart-looking woman whose sage green suit brought out all the richness of her russet hair. Her expression was marred by a frown of boredom.

Standing at the rail beside a small, open sports car were two young men engaged in a desultory conversation. The younger man, in his early twenties, his pale gray eyes in the almost too handsome face, turned toward the lights that were beginning to appear along the shore, was speaking.

". . . had a little time on my hands. Thought I'd give it a whirl. Matter of fact, there's a little bird down here I've been trying to catch for quite a while. Name of Kendrik Haynes. Have you run across her?"

The face of the other man turned colder by degrees. "Yes, I've run into her once or twice. It seems her family used to own the house I live in now." He lit a cigarette, inhaled slowly, then looked at it with dissatisfaction before tossing it over the rail.

"I don't suppose I'll have any trouble finding decent accommodations, will I?" the younger man continued. "It would suit me fine to stay with my little bird, but that may take a bit of doing. I don't suppose you could put me in the way of a place to stay?"

Glacial blue eyes remained unwarmed by the rather grim smile that appeared on the other man's face as he spoke.

"I doubt if you'll find much to suit you this time of year. If you don't mind making your own arrangements for meals, you're welcome to use the extra room at my place."

As the ferry approached the landing slip, the two men nodded briefly to each other and returned to their respective automobiles.

CHAPTER EIGHT

The sigh that escaped Kendrik's lips was mostly of contentment. Only a small, secret sadness shadowed her fine eyes as she looked out over the sandy, windblown couples engaged in the various activities connected with steaming clams and crabs in seaweed and planking the split sides of fish. She had been eager and willing to help, but after doing her share of garnering the largesse of the generous waters, she had watched as, one by one, the subsequent chores were taken over by a laughing twosome. Or a foursome.

Never a threesome or a fivesome, she thought. I'm the odd man out. She looked at Charlie, his salt-encrusted body sprawled in an ungainly heap beside her. "Guess it's you and me, old boy," she whispered, pulling gently on his curly ear.

Later on, an unbelievably large moon rose over the Atlantic and fresh driftwood in the fire shot off flames of blue and green. Several guitars, Kendrik's banjo, a harmonica, and an assortment of voices joined in the creation of a sound that was like a benediction over the group of tired, happy young people. The mellow feeling did not do much, however, to assuage the small, cold feeling of aloneness that was Kendrik's as she looked out over first one couple, then another, their arms entwined, oblivious to all except each other.

Picking up a guitar, she softly chorded alone for a few minutes. The fire had burned lower and flickered its light over the romantic gathering as Kendrik huskily sang several songs. Her eyes strayed slowly out over her friends as drowsy endearments and low, murmured laughter joined the whispers of the surf to the sand in an accompaniment to her music. She lifted her eyes to the darkness beyond the firelit area.

It took several minutes for her eyes to become accustomed to the darkness. When they did, she gasped audibly, a cold shock running through her body. She saw, standing perfectly still just outside the perimeter of light, two men. Kendrik felt the color drain from her face as she looked at the two pairs of eyes that were watching her over the bonfire.

The pale gray eyes revealed little. The absurd thought flashed through her mind. Scott's completely out of context! The burning blue eyes that riveted her own seemed filled with the strangest expression. For a few fleeting seconds she thought she saw tenderness, regret, and longing. It must have been a trick of the firelight, for when she looked again, there was only a sort of chill contempt.

Moving with deliberation to give herself time to recover her equilibrium, she carefully replaced the guitar in its case, closed and snapped it shut before rising to greet the two men as they threaded their way through an assortment of sandy limbs.

"Scott! What on earth are you doing here?"

"Is that any way to greet a lover?" he asked as he grabbed her rigid body close in a rather overdone embrace.

"Scott," she whispered crossly, "Let me go! Why are you—what are you—and with him of all people!"

Scott Chandler stepped back, gray cashmere-clad arms resting on her shoulders. He leaned his brow down to touch her own. "Hey, baby, don't tell me you're not glad to see me. After I came all the way down to this godforsaken place just to tell you I forgive you?" He laughed softly.

"You forgive me!" she exploded, then hastily lowered

her voice. "Never mind that. How did you get to know Marcus? Did he...?"

"Did he what, love?" Scott quirked an eyebrow, a bit of business guaranteed to raise the blood pressure of any woman under fifty-five. "Oh, Manning? I met him on the ferry coming over, and we got to talking. I mentioned I'd come down here to renew our friendship"—malice touched his voice just a little—"and he offered to put me up. Why? What do you care where I stay—or are you making me an offer yourself?"

Kendrik's glance flickered to the tall man who stood with his back to her, talking to Buck Hollis. To her dismay, Marcus turned at that instant, and their eyes locked for a long moment before he turned to Scott.

"You'll be riding with Miss Haynes, so I'll run along now. See you later, Chandler—or maybe not?" His eyes brushed by Kendrik as if she were not there, and he strode off into the darkness.

The party broke up soon afterward with good-natured, lethargic promises to get together again soon.

Both Kendrik and Scott were quiet on the trip back to the village. It was Scott who finally broke the silence by asking where they were going.

"I'm taking you to Marcus's, Scott. It's late, and I really am bushed."

"But we haven't even been alone together yet. We haven't talked at all," Scott protested. "Let's run up to your place for a nightcap."

"No, Scott. Not tonight. In fact, I really don't know why you bothered to come here at all. We finished with all that before. There's no 'friendship' to resume, and I wish you hadn't—" She broke off, not wishing to reveal her anguish at the words he had uttered so casually to Marcus.

"What's the matter, baby? You sound upset over

something. You're not . . . Oh, come on, now! You haven't fallen for Manning, have you?" He laughed in disbelief. "You must be crazy, kid! Why, didn't you know who he is? He's Mark Marksman. You know—big deal television hero, nature boy in person! Come on, honey, even if you were thinking of working out something along those lines, it's no go. He brought along his own special diet with him on the ferry. Mighty tasty-looking dish, too!" Scott slipped an arm around her shoulders, and she promptly shrugged it off.

"Don't be like that, honey. I'll admit I can appreciate a top-drawer redhead when I see one, but you're my own special little wood sprite. You're in a class by yourself!"

"Don't be silly, Scott! Look, we're almost at Marcus's house. I can't take you to the cottage with me at this time of night. I'll drop you off here. Tomorrow Marcus can give you directions to the cottage, and we'll visit a little before you go back."

As Kendrik pulled into the driveway, a single light shone from the back bedroom that used to be Grandy's. She looked at Scott, wondering almost absently what she had found so attractive about him just a few months before.

"Get out, Scott. It's late, and I really don't feel like hassling tonight. It's been a long day." She sighed and gave the man beside her a tired but singularly sweet smile.

Left with little choice, Scott opened the door. Before climbing out of the little car, he reached out a hand and turned her face toward him. After looking at her for several seconds, he gently kissed her on the lips and left.

Driving through the sleeping village, Kendrik was conscious of the fact that she had no intention of starting up anything with Scott Chandler. Any feeling she had had toward that young man had long since evaporated.

CHAPTER NINE

Kendrik was awakened the next morning by the sound of Charlie barking. That meant someone was heading for the cottage. She took time to scramble into her jeans and jersey and was hastily finger-combing her hair as she opened the door to Scott—and Marcus and Vonnie and Erma.

"Good Lord! What a delegation!"

Vonnie hastened to explain. "I was out in the yard when I saw Marcus trying to explain to Scott how to get here, so I offered to show him. Then Marcus said he'd come, too, and Erma came out about then and wanted to know what was going on. So in the end, we all came. I hope you don't mind. It's kind of early, isn't it?" Her voice took on a note of chagrin as she looked at the sleep-flushed face of her friend.

"Well, as long as you're here, come on in. Vonnie, how about making some coffee while I splash ice water on my face and try to wake up. I can't see straight!" Or think straight, or feel straight! Glory be, what a way to start the day!

She hurriedly brushed her teeth and splashed cold water on her face. As she wielded her hairbrush, she tried to create a bit of order in the chaos of her mind. *Marcus is nothing to me. He can't be! And I'm certainly nothing to him. So why do I feel like I'm in a fast elevator going down? Come on, gal, they're only people! Stop quaking in your boots and go out there and play gracious lady. Smile brightly and offer them breakfast.*

As she re-entered the living room, Marcus was leafing through a book of poems by Edna St. Vincent Millay.

59

He looked up. "It opened to 'O World,'" he said. "Is that a special favorite of yours?"

She glanced at Scott and Erma, seated together on the sofa, Scott lighting a cigarette for Erma. Turning toward Marcus, she replied. "It was my mother's favorite. She always said it was a landscape painted with words."

Vonnie brought in coffee. "Couldn't find the sugar, Ken. You still using honey?"

"Yes. I prefer it. Erma? Cream and honey?"

"Black, please." Erma smiled, her face wreathed in blue smoke. "Scott, be a love and hand me my cup, won't you?"

Kendrik looked from Erma to Marcus to Scott to Vonnie. Not a very comfortable group. Vonnie seemed to be the only one of them who remained unaware of the undercurrents.

Marcus was, unexpectedly, the one who broke the tension. "Have you had any luck fishing, Kendrik? I understand the channel bass were running yesterday near the inlet. They caught several at high tide. Why don't we all run down there this afternoon?"

"Mar-cusss! You know you promised me you'd help me with that feature I'm supposed to do for the Sunday issue. If I don't get on it soon, I'll be out of a job!" Erma's usually rather attractive voice took on a note of petulance. "Anyway, you know I don't like fishing!"

Marcus ignored her and continued to look at Kendrik. With no discernible change of expression, he took in her sleep-softened face, the oddly defenseless look in her clear, sea green eyes.

Puzzled at this sudden show of friendliness from the least-expected quarter, she smiled. "I'd love to give it a try. I have some salt mullet we can use for bait."

Suddenly the strain of the past few weeks fell away,

leaving in its stead an atmosphere of peace and warmth. Illogically, Kendrik felt a glow of friendship for each of the four people in the tiny, crowded room. "Come on, Erma," she entreated. "You can write on the next rainy day. Let's not waste this marvelous Indian summer! I'll meet you all there about one or a little after, all right?"

Vonnie stood up. "You four go without me. Buck took a party offshore today, and he won't be back till just before dark. I'm going to work on the shirt I'm making for his birthday."

Marcus looked at Scott. "That suit you, Chandler? Fine. Bring Kendrik and the bait on down to the house after lunch, and we'll go from there. I don't think any of you have a vehicle that can take to the beach too well."

Erma stood and linked her arm in his. "Anything for the visiting firemen, I suppose. We'll see you later."

As the door closed behind therm, Scott opened his arms and said to Kendrik, "Come to me, honey child!"

Kendrik started gathering coffee cups and turned to the kitchen. "Scott, please. We've been through all that. It was fun while it lasted, but nothing more. You know you're not in love with me, and if I started making noises like a bride-to-be, you'd run for your life!" She laughed in a rueful manner. "And if you had anything else in mind, forget it!"

Scott gave an exaggerated sigh, then flashed his boyish smile. "Why do I keep messing my life up with nice women? Why can't I stick to playmates who know how to play by my rules? Like Manning's friend, Erma. Now there's something to warm your hands by on a cold night!" He gave a burlesque leer and sank into the leather lounge chair, his long, elegantly tailored legs extended in front of him.

"You haven't had any breakfast, sleepyhead, and I

haven't had any lunch. Feed the inner man and I might—just might, mind you—help you get your fishing tackle ready. Do you suppose Manning has an extra set of waders I could borrow? I didn't exactly have fishing in mind when I came down here."

The way the beach looked on this particular afternoon would be a memory, Kendrik thought, that she would always be able to take out, like a polished, faceted gemstone, enjoy for a while, then wrap up and put away. The cobalt sky had that intensity peculiar to autumn, and the ocean, though driven to fury near the shore, was deep, sapphire blue out in the distance. Along the glittering stretch of wet sand, an assortment of beach birds vied with each other for choice morsels, while overhead, the gulls commented freely on the small group below.

Standing just out of reach of the spent waves with a surf rod in her hands, Kendrik wrinkled her nose at the distinctive odor of salt mullet. She looked down with distaste at her own attire; blue jeans, windbreaker, cutoff rubber boots. So far, she hadn't even unpacked a dress, since wardrobe space was at a premium in the minute bedroom. Summers spent on this rugged, down-to-earth little island seldom called for more formal attire than she wore at the moment. But looking at Erma, she was suddenly dissatisfied with her own appearance.

Without appearing to do so, she studied the couple standing several yards away from her. Erma's yellow wool pants suit was tucked into tall, slender, wet-look vinyl boots, and her burnished red hair was caught back with a green silk designer scarf. Even Marcus's clothing had that air of being a fabulously expensive copy of ordinary work clothers.

Marcus was laughing down at something Erma had

said as he reeled in his line. He moved off toward the bait box, and Scott edged over to where the two of them had been standing and placed himself beside Erma. Look at the two of them, jockeying for position! You would think Erma was the bait! She wasn't even fishing, either. Just standing there looking revoltingly beautiful as the wind blew her soft wool suit against her body, outlining curves that Kendrik would never have!

After rebaiting his hook with a shiny strip of mullet, Marcus walked down to the edge of the surf, made a long, smooth cast, and began to back up, playing out line as he moved in Kendrik's direction.

She kept her eyes on her own line, conscious of him as he moved into her peripheral vision, of the way the wind whipped his streaked brown hair against his tan forehead, of the way it molded his navy blue nylon jacket to his broad chest and the way the sun glinted on the golden hair on his powerful forearms beneath the turned-back sleeves.

He spoke without turning. "You and Chandler didn't linger long last night. He was in almost as soon as I was. Nothing wrong with love's young dream, is there?

"Oh, don't be ridiculous! There's nothing like that between us!" She heard an echo of her own voice on the night of the hurricane chattering vivaciously to Marcus about Scott Chandler, the man "I'm practically engaged to." How do you get out of that one, my fine-feathered friend?

Suddenly, her rod bent forward! The whine of line stripping off the reel sang out before she could clamp down on the old star drag, the brake that set tension on the line.

"Hook him, girl! Don't let him go!" She had no intention of letting him go.

"How's your drag?" Marcus quickly reeled in his own line and jammed the butt of his rod down in a sand spike. Coming to stand just behind her, he spoke in a low, encouraging voice over her shoulder. "Don't horse him in. He's a big one! You can do it, Kendrik, you can handle him."

The line was stripping out at an alarming rate as she struggled to raise the tip of the rod. The drag had not been set as tightly as she had thought, or perhaps the old reel was just too worn. At any rate, the constant fight to raise the rod, gain a bit of slack, and reel it in quickly just wasn't working! The big bass racing out to sea had other ideas. She was forced, step by step, closer to the edge of the churning water.

"Hang on, honey, he's a keeper!" Scott encouraged. He and Erma stood back and watched as Kendrik was drawn deeper and deeper into the foaming surf, Marcus only a step behind her.

Her arms ached unbearably as she fought the big fish on the other end of the line. Icy water made little impression on her consciousness as it swirled around her legs, dragging boots and heavy denim pants seaward. She braced herself against the heavy pull of the tide and lifted the tip of the rod again, just as the line snapped with a sharp report! Kendrik fell back against Marcus, and both of them were swamped as a tremendous breaker coursed over them.

She was dimly aware of trying to hang on to the surf rod as the rough, tumbling action of tons of cold, surging water beat her down and down, pounding her into the turbulent, sandy bottom. The heavy drag of her wet clothes and the water-filled boots made it impossible for her to regain her feet, and agonizing minutes seemed to go by as she felt herself drawn seaward.

CHAPTER TEN

Struggling up from a frightening void, Kendrik slowly became aware of a comfortable feeling of belonging. Strange. Voices... someone whispering... Grandy? No, not Grandy.

"Kendrik? Sweetheart, can you hear me?" It was Scott. But what on earth was he doing here? A confusion of recent memories overlaid her childhood. She tried to raise her head, but the effort was too great. Her limbs felt enormously heavy as warm darkness closed over her.

Her eyes opened slowly, and she looked around the room, careful not to move her head. She was aware of several things at once: Of a heavy throbbing in her forehead, of an aching feeling of rawness that extended from her throat down into her chest, and of the one dim light that left most of the room in shadow.

A harsh, croaking sound issued from her throat as she tried to call out. Instantly, someone arose from the chair in the corner of the room. Someone tall, whose wide shoulders were silhouetted against the lamplight. She became aware of a new pain as she recognized the grim-looking man beside her bed. Grandy's bed. Grandy's bed?

"What am I doing here?" she managed to whisper.

Marcus leaned over and looked intently into her face. His eyes were red rimmed, and a heavy stubble shadowed his jaw. He looked altogether disreputable... and altogether beautiful. Weakness—it was only that, of course— released the tears from Kendrik's eyes as she looked up at him.

"Lord, woman! I thought I'd lost you!"

65

His words echoed in her mind as she closed her eyes again. She thought she felt a butterfly touch on her lips, but when he spoke again, his voice came from across the room.

"I'll send Vonnie to you," he said, and she heard the door close behind him.

"Oh, Kendrik! What a scare! I hope I never have to live through these last few hours again!" came the anxious voice of her friend. "Scott thought Marcus and you were both goners, and he's not that good a swimmer. Erma was in hysterics, he said, and it was all he could do to comfort her. I think Scott was too embarrassed to stick around once he found out you were going to make it. He's gone, and Erma went with him. Marcus was like a wounded lion! Erma said he grabbed you and held on until he finally managed to drag you to shore, and he wouldn't let anyone else touch you! He made Erma take off her new yellow wool jacket—I think she'd rather have died!—and he wrapped you up in it. And when we saw them pull into the yard here, Scott was driving and Erma was shivering in the seat beside him and Marcus was holding you in the back and both of you were blue!" Vonnie's breath came out in a relieved whistle as she plopped herself into the bedside chair.

Kendrik turned her head, flinching at the pain that accompanied the move. "But why here?" she asked her companion. "How long have I been here, anyway?"

"Hush, honey, don't try to talk yet. You're bound to be raw from all the salt water you swallowed. Well, I guess it just didn't occur to Marcus to take you anywhere else. Mama and I happened to see you all drive up, so we came running over to see what had happened. Scott and Erma filled us in ... mostly Scott. It seemed to me the first thing to do was to get you out of those wet things and into a warm bed. Besides, I guess I still think of you as belonging here. This room was made up, so Marcus said to put you here. He took his own things into the little room across the hall."

Vonnie reached out a comforting hand and held it against Kendrik's cheek for a second. "The funny thing was that Mama—you know Mama, as practical as they come—well, she said it was nonsense when Erma started going on about how people would talk if you stayed here on account of its being improper. Improper! Erma! Can you imagine? Well, Mama told her to stop being silly, that I was going to sleep over here with you, and anyway, we certainly didn't have any room at home with every room overflowing with Erma's things! Oh, you should have seen the look on her face! Erma's, I mean. She just couldn't figure her way out of that one. I mean, she didn't want you over here with Marcus, 'cause she's really got her sights set on him, but she didn't know how to get you out of his house. She's so jealous of you."

Kendrik shook her head. "Oh, no," she croaked. "That's silly! Why, Marcus told me they were—well, sort of . . . together. He said she was a good sport and that they saw a lot of each other before he got engaged." She tried to recall whether or not she should have mentioned Marcus's engagement.

"Yes, Erma told me about Sheila," Vonnie came back. "If you ask me, Erma's getting ready to step into Sheila's shoes. In fact, I wouldn't be surprised if my lover-ly sister hadn't had a hand in the breakup." The rosy glasses of kinship had long ago been broken, as Vonnie had suffered as much as Kendrik under the scathing tongue of Erma.

"Try to relax, honey. I'm going to bring you some hot cambric tea. It'll relax your throat."

Kendrik wanted to ask about Marcus, but the words

would not come. She closed her eyes and slept, tea forgotten.

Sunshine was pouring in through the windows that looked out over the sound when Kendrik once more opened her eyes. She struggled to sit up, and as she looked around, she encountered a strange expression in a pair of intense blue eyes.

Marcus stood up by the chair in the corner of the room, slowly, stiffly, as if he had been sitting a long time. He came closer, nor did his eyes leave her face until he turned abruptly and left the room.

Within minutes, the door reopened to admit Nina O'Neal, Vonnie's mother, bearing a tray.

"Here you are, sweet. Some tea and toast. Let me put this shirt around your shoulders so you won't get chilled." Over her arm she carried a soft, blue flannel shirt that looked enormous. "It could almost be a bathrobe," she laughed as she held it up.

"Thank you, Mrs. O'Neal," Kendrik murmured, pulling the fabric close around her.

As she settled the tray on the girl's lap, Nina O'Neal spoke again, her gentle voice a combination of the typical southern accent and the odd island brogue. "Not that you're any big girl yourself, but Vonnie's so tiny and I'm not much bigger, and our things just wouldn't have been comfortable on you. I put you into one of Marcus's pajama tops and Vonnie tucked hot water bottles around you. After a while, when you get to feeling some stronger, you'd probably like a good, hot bath to wash off some of the salt and sand."

Kendrik was instantly aware of a horrible scratchy stickiness. Her headache was gone, however, and the tea and hot milk toast were doing a lot to assuage the rawness in her throat.

Mrs. O'Neal went on in her brisk, no-nonsense fashion, "Look, Kendrik, honey, I know you'd rather be up at the cottage, but for a few days we think you'd better stay right where you are. The cottage is three miles off, and you just have that one small bedroom. I'd stay up there with you, but I just can't trust this hip of mine. Goes out without a bit of warning. Vonnie has to be over to the Stones' every day to see to old Mrs. Stone. She had a stroke day before yesterday, poor woman, and she's helpless as a softcrab. Thank the Lord for Vonnie. I don't know what this village would do without her, if she is my own girl!" Pride shone in the older woman's face. "She can sleep over here nights, and I'm right next door to pop in and out and Mr. Manning—Marcus—my, he's a fine man, isn't he? He said all he had planned to do was stick to that typewriter of his, and he'd be right in the front room. Just yell for him if you need something and we're not here."

She seemed so pleased with these arrangements that Kendrik hadn't the heart to tell her how she really felt, that the whole idea was impossible! She couldn't just stay in the same house with Marcus, wearing his pajama top, sleeping in the bed he had used. It was Grandy's old sleigh bed with a new foam mattress and down pillow on it—heavenly comfort, but nevertheless, no! It would never do. As soon as possible she must get away from here, away from any possibility of seeing Marcus. Until she learned to school her impressionable heart, to harden herself against his overwhelming attraction, she must avoid him at all costs.

Just before her eyes closed again, she noticed the quilt covering her. It was her mother's crazy quilt. Someone—Marcus?—had retrieved it from the attic floor where she had dropped it ages ago and had carefully spread it over her.

The rest of the day eased by in a blur of sleeping and

drowsy awakenings to tea or soup. Mrs. O'Neal, who brought the trays to her bedside, assured Kendrik it was no trouble.

"Mr. Manning said you'd had a terrific beating by those seas and that you'd be sore for days. Now, you're not to get up until you feel stronger. I've taken to cooking enough for him and bringing over his meals, and it's no trouble to add a little extra for you." She smoothed the pillows and clucked over the girl like a broody hen. "Buck and Vonnie went up to the cottage to be sure everything was turned off and closed up, and they brought Charlie back with them. If you ask me, that old dog's happier down here, anyhow."

If you ask me, I am, too, thought Kendrik.

Marcus didn't come to the room. She heard faint sounds of a typewriter in the distance and, occasionally, voices and the closing of car doors outside. As the numbing tiredness left her limbs and was replaced by a bruised awareness of every muscle in her body, she became more and more restless. She was increasingly aware of the sand that worked its way from her hair to the pillow and then to every inch of the bed.

Nina O'Neal brought an appetizing supper tray, and Kendrik was tempted to ask for help in getting in and out of the tub, but consideration for the older woman's badly healed hip made her decide not to mention it. Vonnie was held up at the Stones', probably. No telling when she would get in. Kendrik was suddenly acutely conscious of being salty, sandy, and sticky to the extent that it overshadowed all her other miseries.

Peering out into the hallway she saw a light coming from the small room at the front of the house that Marcus used as an office. Erratic typing noises and an occasional muttered expletive assured her that he was occupied.

Walking quietly so as not to disturb him, she made her way to the bathroom, where she ran a steaming tub full of water, adding a handful of crystals that swelled into a pine-smelling mass of foam.

Soaking in the steaming, fragrant water went a long way toward restoring her feeling of health, and she worked shampoo through the tangled mass of gritty hair, finally submerging her whole body. Even in the bubbles she was able to swish her hair until it squeaked before she broke through the surface of water once more.

Eyes shut tightly against traces of shampoo, she reached for the towel on the shelf beside the tub where towels were always kept. Or had been! She felt around blindly and encountered nothing except a jar or bottle. Before she could draw back her hand there was a shattering crash! She tried to open her eyes, but the remnants of the shampoo stung them closed. She felt frantically for something on which to dry her face. In desperation she stood up and stepped outside the tub, reaching for the towel rack on the other side of the room. A sharp, piercing pain in her foot caused her to cry out and step back at the same time. Footsteps sounded in the hallway, and she grabbed the shower curtain, wrapping it around her as best she could, just as the door burst open and an angry voice said, "Damn it to hell, woman, you're a disaster! I wish I'd never set eyes on you!"

Standing there in the steamy, pine-scented room, wet hair tumbling over her face and shoulders, eyes shut tight, and plastic curtain clutched around her dripping body, she couldn't see the littered floor, the blood from the cut on her foot staining the linoleum, and the tall, distraught-looking man surveying the scene. Tears slipped down her already wet cheeks, and she felt something dry and soft being pushed into her hand.

Marcus sighed. "Here, wrap yourself in this, and for Pete's sake, don't move your feet! I'm turning my back now, and you can tell me when you're covered."

Kendrik hastened to blot her face so she could open her eyes. She gasped at her first view of the bathroom floor. Looking up at the back of the man standing with his hands on his hips, disapproval in every line of his rigid body, she quickly covered herself in the huge, blue terrycloth wrap and stammered in a choking voice, "I'm—you—I'm ready."

He turned, his withering look searing her from head to toe, and picked her up from where she stood. Stepping quickly into the bedroom, he tossed her onto the bed. "Turn over and cover up in the quilt!" he barked, and as she complied, he grabbed her ankle and held her foot up to the light. "Wait here!" he snapped, as if she had much choice, although at this moment, she would rather have been almost anywhere in the world except here, being frostbitten by icy blasts from this man's temper.

Hands closed around her ankle again as he murmured, "This is going to hurt. Be still!"

Something cold touched her skin briefly, then the sharp smell of disinfectant and a stinging sensation.

"Ouch!" She rolled over and sat as he stood up and glared down at her. His eyes were black with some kind of emotion. Anger, she supposed.

"Put on some clothes. I want to talk to you!" He turned and was gone, slamming the door behind him.

For a full minute, Kendrik sat where he had left her, speechless with rage, frustration, and humiliation. Then, catching her breath, she yelled after him, "I hate you! I hate you, do you hear me? I'm leaving right now, and I never want to see you again!" She jumped off the bed, wincing as her cut foot felt the pressure of her weight.

Openly sobbing, she snatched up her suitcase and threw into it whatever she could readily lay her hands on of her possessions. Pulling the flannel nightgown on and shoving her feet into floppy slippers, for whoever had brought her things from the cottage had brought no other clothes, she marched out of the bedroom, flinging the door back against the wall. Without looking to the left or the right, she stormed out of the front door. She paused in the front yard to look frantically for her car, but it was not in sight.

Too angry to do anything else, she started walking in the direction of the cottage. Fortunately, at that time of night the villagers were not awake to see the fiery-eyed girl clad in a flapping white flannel gown, her hair streaming behind her and her tiny suitcase swinging in her hand as she strode through the darkened street like an avenging angel.

She passed the O'Neals' house, all windows dark. The grocery store was long since closed. Her long, angry stride ate up the distance between her goal and the man she was escaping, and she had passed the village and was on the open stretch leading to the woods, her steps beginning to drag now, when she first heard the low whine of an engine behind her.

There was no place to hide—not a bush or a rock broke the flatness of the terrain. Her foot was aching now, her crocheted slippers long since lost in the sand that encroached on the narrow strip of paving. Making an effort to disguise her limp, she held her head high and did not slow her pace as the vehicle pulled up beside her. The door opened as it crept along in low gear.

"Get in!" ordered the voice from the dark interior. She ignored it and walked on.

"Look, I've had just about all I can take from you! You get in here, or I get out and put you over my knee and whale the daylights out of you!"

Kendrik stood irresolute for a moment, then, sighing, she climbed up onto the high seat. She didn't look at the man beside her, and after a moment of silence, he tossed a cigarette from the window, downshifted, and moved off in the direction of the cottage. Neither of them spoke until he pulled into the tree-shadowed driveway.

Taking her suitcase, she opened the door and stepped out quickly, before he could help her, and her voice, as she grudgingly thanked him, was barely audible. As she climbed the steps to the porch, more tired than she cared to admit, she heard him get out and follow her up. He opened the door, reached in and turned on the lights, and stood back for her to pass.

All the fight was gone out of her now, and she felt like nothing so much as sinking into dark oblivion. The harsh overhead light in the small room shone down on her, revealing deep violet shadows under her dulled eyes, the complete lack of color in her face adding to her look of utter defeat. A bruise marked her brow, fading into her hairline and reminding the man who stood silently studying her of the terrible battering she had taken under tons of water before he had regained his feet and dragged her to safety.

With an inarticulate sound, he reached out and drew her into his protective arms. He pressed her face against his broad chest as he stroked her hair, murmuring soft, broken words over her head.

Kendrik drew a long, shuddering sigh and was still, committing herself utterly to the reality of his strength. There was no passion in his embrace, only an overwhelming tenderness. After a while, she looked up, searching his face for some sign, her own terrible vulnerability naked in her eyes. Immediately, she felt him stiffen, and he released her.

"I'm going away. Away from the island." The words lay starkly there between them.

"But why? I thought you were going to be here for at least two years. What's wrong?" She felt as if something precious, almost within her grasp, had slipped away.

He turned away and spoke in a harsh, strained voice. "Kendrik, I just can't stick around here anymore. It's too small an island for the two of us not to run into each other constantly."

"But why is that—" she started, but he interrupted.

"Look, you're what?—twenty-two? You're a baby! A sweet, well-brought-up young lady. Too damned attractive, I'll be the first to admit that, but what you need is to marry some decent young fellow who'll give you a home and a houseful of babies. You can join the PTA and be a Cub Scout leader and play bridge with the other young wives and go to an occasional dance at the club. That's the kind of life you need, not getting tangled up with someone who's old enough to be your... uncle!"

The bleakness on his face was supplanted by a look of bitterness, of cynicism, as he continued. "I'll be moving around too much to settle down anywhere for long, and if I get lonely maybe I'll look up a few old friends from my wilder days. You'd be amazed how many good-looking women there are in the television industry." He still hadn't looked at the girl who was standing there, still as death, with a stricken look on her face. "The keys to the house will be at the O'Neals'. Get your things or leave them. It makes no difference to me, one way or another."

He turned to her now, but quickly looked away as he continued speaking. It was almost as if he forced the words from him, forced the cruelty that twisted the knife. "I understand Central America can be pretty exciting this time of year. Maybe Erma and I could wangle a joint assignment down there. I don't think I'd have any trouble persuading her to go along, do you?"

Kendrik still had not spoken, and Marcus dared one intent look in her direction, a look that held something Kendrik had never before seen in his eyes. Then it was gone, the familiar shutters again closing over the blue flame.

She was still standing there in the middle of the room, the suitcase lying where it had dropped from her nerveless fingers, when the sound of his car faded into the distance.

CHAPTER ELEVEN

It was almost noon when Kendrik heard two cars drive up into her driveway.

Using work as a palliative, she had taken down all the screens and was washing the outsides of the windows. She looked down from the ladder on which she was perched and waved to the three people approaching. Only someone who knew her extremely well would have been able to detect the pain and shock beneath the smile she gave them.

Buck Hollis indicated the pleasant-looking young man beside him. "You remember my brother Jeff, don't you, Kendrik?" He put his hand on the shoulder of the rather serious looking individual. "He was supposed to be at the beach party, but something came up and he didn't make it. Jeff, you remember Kendrik Haynes. She used to visit her grandfather, Cap'n Dick, next door to the O'Neals."

Jeff smiled up at Kendrik, his dark gray eyes rather warm in his bony, attractive face. "It has been a long time since I've seen you, though. I guess because you were here mostly in the summer and these last years I was away working."

"What do you do—or did you do?" Kendrik asked, immediately chiding herself for presuming to ask questions before she even acknowledged the introduction. She stepped to the ground and, wiping her hands, led the way into the cottage. She went directly to the kitchen and put the kettle on to boil, then turned to her guests and bade them sit down.

"I did do most anything that came to hand to earn my tuition," Jeff said, answering her question. "I'm a teacher now, sort of. With a bit of welfare worker thrown in for

77

good measure." His glance moved around the room admiringly, obviously appreciating the way in which Kendrik's excellent taste and individual flair had made the little cottage a real home.

"By the way," Vonnie said, "did I tell you that we took your car to the beach the day after you got swamped and searched for your surf rod? There was just the barest chance that it had washed ashore, but no such luck. Then, when I got back to Marcus's he said you had decided to come on home because he was planning to go away. That was pretty sudden, wasn't it?" She looked searchingly at her friend. "He's gone. He left early this morning on the first ferry, and he told Mama he didn't have any idea when he'd be back."

Kendrik briskly set out the makings for sandwiches and poured the coffee. "You may as well join me for lunch. Not bad, and there's plenty of it, such as it is, as Grandy always said." Turning to Jeff, she asked, "What do you mean, a sort of teacher?"

He spread horseradish sauce on his brown bread. "Well, you see, there are lots of kids in my regular classes who come from broken or shaky homes where nobody really cares enough for them to give them any decent standards. They're not juvenile delinquents—at least, not yet—but most of them have lived with anger, with hostility and frustration and worse for so long, they don't know anything else. They're not even aware that there are any alternatives!"

His concern with these children was evident in his demeanor. "There are plenty of people who live lives of—well, of love and kindness, in a sort of harmony with themselves. And, really, it's mostly in your attitude toward life. These kids have to be shown that it's within their power to change this pattern for themselves. It isn't easy. They're still stuck in their home environment for now, but I try to give them something to shoot for, show them that not all the world is like their little corner and that they can make it out of there if they try hard enough!" He laughed in an embarrassed manner. "Pardon the preaching. I carry a soapbox with me."

"No, really. I'm interested," Kendrik responded. "Please go on. How do you show them?"

"Well, I'm taking a small group home with me over the holidays. Thank the Lord for an understanding family! I've done it twice now. Some wins, some draws, and probably a few losses. It's not the sort of thing you can evaluate in a short while—takes years."

They discussed Jeff's venture at length over lunch, and both Buck and Vonnie were quick to notice Kendrik's interest. Buck was the first to mention it.

"Have you ever worked with kids, Kendrik? The reason I asked, Jeff had some trouble last year with some of the older girls, and he may need a helping hand if he gets girls again. Our family's mostly geared to boys."

Vonnie encouraged her, seeming to sense a need in her friend for something into which to pour her young energies. Both Buck and Vonnie had been aware of a growing tension between Marcus and Kendrik, and it didn't take a particularly observant person to see that she had sustained some sort of shock. No doubt it was connected with Marcus's hasty departure, for Buck knew definitely that as little as a week ago Marcus hadn't been planning a trip in the near future.

Before driving off in Buck's old sedan, leaving the Bluebird they had returned behind, it was agreed upon to get together before the children arrived and discuss ways and means of coping with the assortment of ages, sexes, and dispositions.

Jeff was the only one of the three who remained unaware of the need Kendrik had to lose herself in some activity that would absorb her both physically and mentally.

As winter gradually cast its shadow over the island, the native islanders seemed to draw closer together. Perhaps it was a feeling of being alone at last as the last visiting fisherman put away his tackle and caught the ferry to the mainland.

The island men, some in small open boats and some in larger cabin cruisers, still fished the waters of the sound and the ocean, but the pace was slower. The hard, wet nor'easters inclined the men to spend more time mending nets in the tall, bare net sheds or sitting around a red-hot cast-iron stove talking in a desultory fashion of seasons past while curls of soft juniper fell from busy barlows.

The women gathered in twos and threes in steamy kitchens, needing more of an excuse than the men for a gossipy get-together, but the traditional borrowed cup of sugar was soon forgotten as they settled down to the vital business of exchanging ideas and information. Not that there were many details left undiscovered in a community of this size, but the coming together seemed somehow to strengthen the men and women whose families had dared the forces of nature for generations on this bare little strip of land.

Kendrik, Vonnie, Buck, and Jeff, along with several others of their age group, managed to get together frequently. Sometimes the small cottage in the woods rang with the music of guitars, and more than once they borrowed one of the big net sheds for an impromptu square dance.

Simple pleasures that managed to keep at bay, almost,

the throbbing ache that caught Kendrik unaware at unexpected times. She avoided as much as she could passing the house on the southern end of the island, its battened storm-blinds somehow reminding her too much of the guarded look she had surprised more than once on Marcus's face.

Sometimes Vonnie would see her look up suddenly at the sound of a four-wheel-drive vehicle, and expression of excitement quickly come and as quickly go on her face.

Thanksgiving came around, and Kendrik shared baked goose with the O'Neals. Nina O'Neal laughingly confessed that the goose that looked so fine and brown had been a long time in the stew pot before he ever saw the inside of her oven.

"Howard wouldn't have his goose any other way but stewed, for he always wanted rutabagas, potatoes, and piebread in his gravy, but Erma thinks that's too country. She says the only proper way to cook fowl is to bake it?"

"I'd like to see her get a fork into this bird without parboiling it first! Anyway, what does she know about cooking?" Vonnie poured the rich gravy over her pone bread. "She can't even make toast in an automatic toaster!"

"Now, Vonnie—" Her mother's voice was softly reproving, but her smile was understanding. "You know Erma never did enjoy spending the time in the kitchen that you did—but then, she's always been so pretty."

Kendrik's thoughts veered uncontrollably in a dangerous direction. She had made no inquiries as to the whereabouts of the oldest O'Neal girl, for she didn't think she could bear to be certain of what she only surmised. She busied herself serving the slices of pumpkin pie topped with mounds of whipped cream.

As Christmas approached, Kendrik considered accepting the invitation from her father and Grace to visit them in Texas. She was tempted; the only real problem was Charlie, older now and bothered by his winter malady, arthritis.

Don't lie to yourself, stupid girl! You know Vonnie would keep Charlie for you. You don't want to leave because of Marcus, of course. This is the only place you've ever known him, and he's more real somehow on the island—on the beach, where you first saw him, here in this room, where he held you in his arms. Oh, damn, damn, damn! When would it stop hurting!

Jeff's group of children came, four boys and a girl between the ages of nine and thirteen. Kendrik went with him to meet them at the ferry.

The weather that day was rough, a sleety rain that made the ferry trip less than enjoyable for the five youngsters. They were resentful at being passed around, afraid of these raw, new surroundings, and ill-at-ease with strange adults. Drawing close together as if to ward off attack from a new front, they presented a poignant picture to Kendrik, who covered her feelings with a brisk friendliness as she and Jeff shepherded the silent little group into Jeff's rusty old station wagon.

"This the best car you c'n afford?" sneered one of the older boys as they bounced along the rough blacktop. "We got better'n this at my pa's place."

"Yep. This is the best I can afford." Jeff grinned over his shoulder. "It used to be in a little better condition, but cars don't last long down here. Salt, you know."

The boy lapsed back into silence, a slightly puzzled look on his face.

Kendrik and Jeff carried on an intermittent, low-key

conversation, not shutting the children out with their comments, but demanding no response of them either. It had been agreed on beforehand that there could be no hard sell of the values they wished to impart, for these children must return to their own environment. The real benefit, if any, must come from exposing these children to everyday living among people who, while short of financial blessings, were rich in loving kindness and simple goodness.

She recalled Jeff's telling her of his early exposure to a teacher with a strong bent for social work. This man had made a strong, lasting impression on the young boy who didn't fit the family mold of fisherman, but who hadn't a pattern to follow until then.

The rest of the day flew by, with all of Jeff's and Kendrik's imagination occupied with trying to settle the youngsters into the community. The boys were to stay at the Hollises, big barnlike home. There had been five Hollis boys, all of whom were grown now and all but the two youngest, Buck and Jeff, with homes of their own.

"This house is a regular boy's dormitory, and I've not forgotten how to handle a bunch of boys with one hand tied behine me," reminded the kind, blustery Mrs. Hollis.

Lisa, the silent nine-year-old girl, with her cotton-blonde hair and round, dark eyes, was a bit more of a problem. Kendrik was more than willing to make room for the painfully shy little girl, but it remained for Nina O'Neal to win her over.

"I declare, I don't know what I'm going to do about those kittens," she said to Kendrik in the child's hearing. "I've got this bad hip, and it's more than I can do to keep chasing them down. They're right at the troublesome age now. Cute, though, cute as buttons!"

Lisa's large eyes grew even larger as she sidled up close

beside the attractive, gray-haired woman. "Do you really have some live kittens? In the house? Won't they mess up the floor and tear up the curtains and leave filthy fleas in the beds?" Her words reminded Kendrik of verses learned by heart from repetition.

"Prob'ly, child, prob'ly, but I don't mind so long as I can find somebody willing to help me keep up with the little scamps."

As Kendrik watched the woman and the child walk away, both considering the best way to keep the kittens from getting stepped on, she thought of what Jeff had told her about Lisa's background: parents separating after a nine-and-a-half-year battle, house being repossessed, neither parent willing to take the child, who went from foster home to foster home, becoming more and more silent.

Her thoughts jumped back to a golden afternoon in the attic of an old house—"There was nothing to come for, no home to come to"—and to the little living room of her cottage, where Marcus had told her of two basically fine people, totally unsuited and hacking away at each other morning, noon, and night.

So many victims, she thought. I can almost see why he's so adamant about not getting married. But, oh, how I want him! If only he could be satisfied with the little I have to offer, I would follow him wherever he wanted to go. I would love him enough for both of us and teach him to trust again!

The image of a lovely, well-dressed redheaded woman forced its way to the front of her mind. Someone like Erma would be a marvelous hostess. She would be at home with the television and the publishing people he would associate with on the mainland and would always know just what to wear and what to say. Visions of Erma in her clinging pink jumpsuit, in the chiffon cocktail dresses Vonnie had described to her, in filmy, lacy lingerie, pushed their way into her mind. She tried to visualize Erma in a housedress and an apron, but couldn't.

Calling Charlie, Kendrik reached for her old windbreaker and stepped into her boots. As they headed for the beach, it occurred to her that Marcus had never even seen her in a dress.

Jeff fell into the habit of bringing the children out to the cottage every afternoon. He would pile the boys into the rusty old station wagon, pick up Lisa at the O'Neals, and drive the three miles to where Kendrik awaited with hot chocolate and whatever her oven had produced that morning. The children were completely at ease now and often engaged the two adults in their rowdy games, with slightly hysterical results.

They had music. All the children were enthralled by Kendrik's seemingly endless repertoire of songs. She taught them to sing nonsense songs that had them helpless with laughter long before they finished all the verses. On these occasions, Jeff, whose pleasant bass voice simply couldn't follow a melody, sat back and watched the group surrounding the lovely, green-eyed girl with the guitar.

Misgivings niggled at her mind more than once when she caught a certain expression in his steady, gray eyes. She pushed them to the back of her mind, intent on making these last few days of the children's visit memorable.

They cooked chocolate fudge and fought over who was to scrape out the pan. She took them into the woods and showed them how to collect yaupon twigs and leaves, which they then washed, chopped, and parched in the oven. Not knowing the outcome of this venture beforehand, they were delighted when she removed the nondescript brown leaves from the oven and with them brewed a delicious tea. As they drank the infusion, liberally laced with honey, she told them how the Indians used to come each year from the mountains and the piedmont to trade flintstones for a supply of the leaves to make the tea they called the black drink.

Two days before Christmas, Vonnie brought Lisa to the cottage with her tiny plastic suitcase.

"Guess who turned up this morning, bright and early?" she said wryly. "None other than my favorite—and only—sister!"

Kendrik's mind did a hasty about-face. "But I thought she was... Isn't she in Central America?"

"Wha-a-at? Where did you get that idea?"

"Oh, I don't know," Kendrik said. "Somehow I got the impression that she had planned a trip down there. In connection with her work, maybe."

"Well, I don't know where you picked that up, but you sure are off base! Remember, she left here with your boy friend, Scott Chandler? I don't know whose idea it was, but they headed for the mountains for a ski resort, some place near Blowing Rock, I think. Anyhow, they met some friends of his who were going on a cruise to the Bahamas—bloody swank!"

"You mean that's where she's been all along?"

"Why this sudden interest in Erma? But, yes, at least that's where she was till the cruise ended. According to her, the marriage of the couple who owned the yacht almost ended, too!" Her derisive tone of voice left Kendrik in no doubt as to her opinion of this unknown group. "She looks great, though! Redheads usually don't tan, but Erma goes at it in a slow, sure way and comes out looking like a million! I tried it her way one summer, but I just freckle, no matter how I do it!"

As Vonnie caught her breath after this verbal barrage, Kendrik directed her attention away, anxious to disguise the effect of Vonnie's disclosure. Her eyes fell on the child who was lying on the floor beside the old dog, talking softly into his scarred, brown ear.

"You'll feel better when warm weather comes again. My grandmama has arth-ur-ritis, too, and she lives in a hotel in Florida. It's always warm there. Maybe you can go to Florida, too."

Kendrik smiled and shook her head gently at the little girl. "I'm afraid not, honey. This is the only place Charlie and I have, and it happens to be on the cold side of the island. That's why I let him stay inside in the coldest weather."

"Why is it the coldest?" inquired the child.

"Well, it's on the northwest end of the island, and when the winter wind comes whipping down from the north, the first thing it hits on this stretch of the banks is my cottage."

"But isn't there a warm side of the island where you could take him?" Lisa persisted.

Kendrik thought of her grandfather's old house on the southern shore, protected by the bulk of the village and by the island itself. " 'Fraid we have to do the best we can with what we have, honey," she said gently.

Later that night, with the small, thin girl asleep beside her, Kendrik lay awake and let her thoughts roam down trails she had not allowed herself to explore for weeks.

Erma was not with Marcus! From what Vonnie had divulged, she had not been anywhere near Central America! But then, maybe Marcus hadn't, either. What if they had been together on the cruise? It was entirely possible that Marcus knew these same people, that he had been included as a friend of Erma's.

She speculated wildly on the possibilities as she realized how little she actually knew of his life away from the island—or on it, for that matter. How can I love him so much and know so little about him? she asked herself.

The answer flowed through her consciousness; I know the feel of his lips in kissing. I know the touch of his hands in gentleness and the sound of his voice in anger and in tenderness. I know that I've been marking time with my life until he came along and if he doesn't want me, I don't think I can exist. And he doesn't want me! The pain that flooded her heart was as keen as it had been on the night he walked away from her.

Christmas morning dawned cold and clear. It had always been a rather quiet holiday on the island. There were no shops to cater to Christmas shoppers, only the general store and the mail-order catalogs. There were no streets to decorate, even if the wind would have allowed the decorations to remain. Homes and the plain white church were decorated with wreaths and trees of cedar, pine, and the red-berried yaupon.

Kendrik, Jeff, and Vonnie had helped the children make ornaments from pine cones, sea shells, and the lids of tin cans, fringed around the edges with heavy shears and centered with pictures cut from old Christmas cards.

Jeff had brought the children each day to practice with Kendrik a song she had taught them. With the guitar, some bells, a homemade drum, and combs and tissue paper, the little band rehearsed as assiduously as the largest choir. The song, an eighteenth-century English ballad that was one of Kendrik's favorite Christmas carols, was to be the children's gift to the families who had opened their homes to them.

Lisa and Kendrik were dressed and ready long before it was time to go to the Hollises', where they were to join the O'Neals for Christmas dinner. Kendrik had trimmed Lisa's wispy, unkempt hair so that fluffy bangs broadened her thin little face. She brushed it until it shone, then tied it up into a topknot with a crocheted band.

Lisa helped Kendrik unpack her own dresses, and together they decided that Kendrik should wear a long cotton in cranberry red. Kendrik admitted to herself that it felt good to wear a dress for a change. She thought of Marcus and wished he could see her.

The children's song was enthusiastically received, and they, in turn, were pleased with the homemade toys they were given. Mrs. O'Neal had made Lisa's doll, and Kendrik had dressed it from her own supply of quilting scraps. The boys all got whittled boats of surprisingly complex design.

All through the huge meal, Kendrik was aware of Jeff's eyes on her. She had purposely avoided being alone with him lately, by instinct if not conscious design.

When Vonnie arose and began to clear away the dishes, Kendrik joined her, and soon the girls were up to their elbows in hot, sudsy dishwater.

They spoke little, each content with her own thoughts. As they began to put away the lovely old china, Vonnie was the first to break the silence.

"You know how Jeff feels about you, don't you?"

Kendrik started almost guiltily. "Oh, Vonnie...no! He's so nice, and I like him so very much. No, he hasn't actually said anything, but—"

"He will. Ken? What about it? Are you still crazy about Marcus?" Then, as Kendrik would have protested, Vonnie said, "Oh, yes, I'm not stone blind. I don't know what happened between you two, but I do know you haven't been the same ever since he left."

Both girls looked up as the kitchen door opened to admit Jeff Hollis.

"Buck wants you, Vonnie. I'll help Kendrik finish up in here."

Vonnie cast an almost pleading look at her friend as she removed her apron and placed it in Jeff's hand.

Kendrik turned back to the pile of pots and pans in the dishpan. "I think they enjoyed it, don't you?" she chattered brightly. "Wonder why Erma didn't come? Vonnie said she was home."

Jeff gave a small chuckle. "I wouldn't think this was Erma's idea of a Christmas party, would you?"

Kendrik could think of nothing to say as she felt the tension increase between her and the quiet man standing so close beside her.

Very deliberately, he reached out and lifted Kendrik's hands from the hot water. He dried them silently on the apron Vonnie had previously handed him, and still holding her hands in his own strong, sensitive hands, he spoke softly.

"Kendrik, don't pretend you don't know what's on my mind. I—we haven't known each other very long, but it's been plenty of time for me to know. You're not blind—I can't hide the way I feel about you, Kendrik. Buck and Von guessed, and even the boys have ribbed me about it! Ken, darling, could you...is there a chance...?" His voice died away as he saw the dismay on her lovely face.

"Oh, Jeff...no. I care so much, but just not that way." She saw the naked pain on his face, and her heart wept. "It just wouldn't work. I can't explain," she whispered.

Not speaking for a moment, Jeff searched the concerned eyes so close to his own, then leaned down and gently touched her lips with his. "Oh, well"—the grin didn't quite hide the bleak look on his face—"nothing ventured, nothing gained."

CHAPTER TWELVE

After the children returned to the mainland, accompanied by Jeff, who cut short his holiday, time once more began to drag for Kendrik. Cold, lashing rains kept her housebound for days on end, and her eyes protested long hours of quilting, crocheting, and reading. She taught herself several new songs, but music became more of a chore than a joy as her eyes kept straying toward the village and her thoughts to the tall, angry, cold-eyed, harsh-voiced, utterly desirable man called Marcus.

It's funny, she mused to herself, Scott, Jeff, all the perfectly charming men I've dated, danced with, laughed with, even kissed, they're like the paper dolls I used to play with in Grandy's attic. No, the paper dolls had more substance. And this—this man! This great beast of a man makes my bones turn to jelly when I even think about being in his arms—his strong, brown, golden-haired arms, warm with the smell of pipe tobacco and sunshine!

The picture of Marcus as he had looked that day in the attic swam before her eyes. Almost without volition, Kendrik walked into the bedroom and took her heavy russet coat from the wardrobe. Shrugging into it, she picked up her canvas-and-leather handbag and went out to the car.

Even as she neared the village, she would not admit to herself where she was going. It was as if something outside her own mind and body were directing her. Passing the store, she pulled up in front of the O'Neals' house. Nina O'Neal answered her knock, opening the door with a smile on her round freckled face, her graying hair awry.

"Why, Kendrik! Come in, come in. I'd just about given you up, it's been so long."

"I can't stay, Mrs. O'Neal. I just wanted to pick up the keys to next door. I left some trunks and things in the house, and I thought I'd get them out of the way before Mr. Manning comes back."

"Have you heard from him then? We've not heard a word, even Erma, and she was trying to find out where he was. She asked at the newspaper office, and they didn't know where he'd got to!" Mrs. O'Neal drew Kendrik into the warm, fragrant kitchen. "Just let me find where I put those keys. Hot enough in here, isn't it?" She laughed. "I'm putting up a few jars of Brunswick stew. It's silly, when I have to go into my freezer to get the vegetables, but I do like having a few jars on hand for emergencies. You can say what you will about freezers, but a good pantry full of canned goods won't worry you to death every time the power goes off." She handed Kendrik the keys. "Don't bother about returning them if you forget. I have another set, and you can just drop them off next time you're by here."

Kendrik sat outside the Manning house for several minutes, just looking. There was something sad about an uninhabited house, especially in a January rain. Brushing aside the touch of sadness, she restarted the car and pulled it around to the back yard, as close to the back door as possible, thinking of the rain and the heavy trunk and box.

Locating the proper key, she unlocked the back door and stepped inside. Hmmm. Musty. Closed up too long in damp weather. Old Miss Tull would have a fit! What's it to me? Kendrik thought suddenly. Why should I care if his whole house disappears in a cloud of mildew?

But something, some secret little urge, made Kendrik walk through the kitchen, past the stairway to the attic, down the dark, narrow hallway to the door of the small room on the left. This was the room Marcus had slept in while she was there. Opening the door, she turned on the light against the gloom and looked around. Nothing. There was no feeling of anyone's ever having inhabited the bare little room. She walked over to the closet and opened the door. No clothes. A few old wire hangers... nothing.

Kendrik was secretly aghast at her own behavior in deliberately invading Marcus's home. The fact that it had once been her grandfather's didn't excuse the act. But as she turned off the lights in the chilly room, wondering idly as she did why Marcus had failed to have the power cut off before he left, she sighed in resignation and turned to the other door. Marcus's door. Her door. Grandy's door.

An overwhelming surge of pain in the region of her heart struck her as she stood in the doorway, one hand still on the china doorknob, and took in the scene before her.

The bed she had left so tumbled—his bed—was not as she had left it. The quilt had been neatly spread, though the pillow was still indented where her head had lain—or was it his head? Across the foot of the bed, carefully folded, was the blue terrycloth robe of his that she had worn so briefly.

Walking slowly, almost reluctantly, over to the big mahogany wardrobe, she opened the doors. Hanging rather forlornly inside were two blue chambray shirts, a worn tweed jacket, and beside them, on a single hanger, the clothes she had worn that afternoon so long ago—the blue jeans with the flower embroidery, the old, faded rose top, even, she saw with embarrassment, the skimpy little panties and bra. All were neatly washed. By Mrs. O'Neal, no doubt.

She reached out a tentative hand and touched the gray

tweed jacket. As the hangers jangled beneath her fingers, a waft of scent reached her, the odor of aftershave, of tobacco, and—sunshine?

Suddenly overcome by a rush of emotion, Kendrik turned and threw herself across the bed, sobbing uncontrollably. Out poured all the love, the longing, the loneliness of the past few months. The tears she had not shed, the tears she had sublimated into long, solitary walks, into music played for one who couldn't hear it, tore from her body now. She wept hopelessly for a long time, and as the shuddering sobs diminished, she sank into a deep, exhausted sleep.

Hours later she was aroused slowly from an almost comatose state. At first, her only impression was one of terrible coldness. The dampness of the unheated house had permeated her body, and as she tried to sit up in the darkened room, she trembled uncontrollably. What had awakened her? There had been something just outside the reaches of her mind . . . a sound?

Extending a shaky hand toward the bedside lamp, she inadvertently knocked against something and sent it crashing to the floor.

Within seconds, a shadowy form filled the open doorway, and a deep, achingly familiar voice demanded, "Who's there?"

Too stunned to move, she felt as if a hand had closed over her heart, squeezing the blood from it. "Marcus." The slight whisper reached the man's ears, and he moved swiftly to the bed.

"Kendrik?" he asked in disbelief. "What the—what are you doing here? How long have you been here?" He sat down on the bed suddenly, as though his legs could no longer support his weight.

The shock of seeing this man had rendered Kendrik mute, and she could only peer at him through the darkness, shivering violently now with something besides cold.

"What is it, child?" he demanded. "Say something!" He reached out a hand and found her own in the darkness. "You're like ice! Kendrik, how long have you been here? Will you please tell me what's going on?" he insisted. He stood up and lifted her from the bed, cradling her in his arms as though she were a baby.

"Come into the living room. The fire's burning in there, and we must thaw you out!" He looked down on her face as they neared the lighted room, his eyes probing her own enormous eyes, still dark with emotion, and his gaze moved swiftly over the pale, sharply defined cheekbones to the trembling mouth.

Kendrik had not spoken since that first uttered cry of recognition. Still studying her intently, he was aware of several things at once. Of the slightly swollen eyelids and the tear-stained cheeks, of the look of ... was it maturity? Sadness? A look of complete vulnerability.

Gently he led her inside, still not releasing her, but holding her arm as though afraid she would slip away. Wordlessly, they searched each other's faces. Then, with a soft curse under his breath, Marcus crushed her to him, and with a sigh, Kendrik surrendered her soul to this man she loved beyond all else.

For a long time she was content to draw from his warm strength, to experience unutterable bliss as he held her chilled and trembling body in his arms.

She became aware of the heavy pounding of his heart beneath her head. His hands moved up her back and captured her hair in a gentle grasp. He slowly tipped her head back, his lips hovering over her own for a breathtaking moment before they settled in a kiss of such overwhelming tenderness that Kendrik was shaken to the depths by her love. It was all she could do to remain silent, to still the fluttering of her heart. Some small voice inside her cried out a warning, attempted to push forward her pride, but Kendrik surrendered to the utter bliss of the moment.

The sounds of laughter and a passing vehicle came as a dash of icy water over the two people in the lamplit room. Drawing apart with a look of consternation, both turned at the same time toward the window. Nothing moved outside in the pre-dawn stillness, but from a distance came the fading noise of a truck as it pulled up to the nearby wharves.

"Early fishermen," Marcus said in an expressionless voice as he stepped back. "Just what I needed on top of everything else!"

The coldness so recently swept away by Marcus's warmth crept over Kendrik once more. "What do you mean?" she whispered, feeling suddenly bereft.

Turning abruptly toward her where she stood beside the undraped window, Marcus ran shaking fingers through her tumbled brown hair. "Why the hell did you have to be here, lying in wait to spring your little trap!" he demanded. "I thought I'd be safe, staying away this long, but no, no sooner do I return than you set up a sweet little scene in the early hours of the morning. Before a window, yet! Well, I hope to hell you're satisfied!"

Kendrik stared at the shadowed planes of his face, now marred by bitterness. "Marcus, don't," she beseeched. "Please don't say that." She took a deep breath as the room seemed to darken before her eyes. The last shimmering image she saw before blackness closed over her was bitterness giving way to concern as Marcus moved swiftly toward her.

When she came to, she was in his arms once more, this time on the sofa. It had been only a momentary collapse, no doubt brought on by the erratic course of her emotions in the past hours—from the depths of grief to a freezing sleep to the shock of seeing Marcus and the thrill of his tender kisses. Something in her had balked at being plunged into the depths again, and her mind had resisted in the quickest way.

Remembrance made her sit up abruptly in his arms. His terrible accusations lay between them like a burning sword. She tried to move away, feeling as insecure as if she were on quicksand, but he caught her close again.

"No, my dearest . . . no, no. There's no point in trying to run away . . . for either of us." His words were spoken tenderly, with overtones of resignation, of sadness.

Kendrik looked up into his face, trying desperately to find some clue, some reason for the sudden change in him.

He moved her gently from his lap, pulling the woolen lap rug over her as he stood up. "You need some brandy. As a matter of fact, so do I." His slightly unsteady voice strove for lightness as he turned toward the handsome cabinet and poured two drinks. "Drink it," he commanded, handing her one of the delicate, stemmed glasses. "Go on, it's what you need now to steady you and warm you up. We have to talk, Kendrik, and the sooner the better, I suppose." He sat down on one end of the sofa and extended an arm along the back.

She shuddered as the fiery liquid touched her throat and carefully placed the glass on the slab of monkeypod wood that served as a coffee table. "Where do we start? I simply don't understand what's happening, Marcus. I feel like I've been riding a roller coaster blindfolded. Won't you please start from the beginning and tell me what's going on? No, don't touch me now," she said as he clasped her shoulder.

"You're right. We won't get much talking done that way." He sighed and leaned forward, his forearms resting on his muscular thighs, his eyes staring into his glass as though it was a crystal ball soon to reveal all the answers. After a while he started to speak in a deep, thoughtful voice. "From the moment I first saw you, Kendrik, I couldn't get you out of my mind. There's something about you. I don't know what it is. You make me overreact! I always end up wanting to shake you or make love to you!" He cast a quick look in her direction without turning his head. "I've told you I'm too old for you. I'm thirty-two and you're still only a child—"

She interrupted softly. "I'm not a child, Marcus. Not anymore. I'm twenty-three now, and I feel a hundred."

He continued. "Anyhow, I knew I had to get away. I had an idea you were becoming physically attracted to me. Oh, I'm not bragging about it." She tried to interrupt, but he went on speaking. "I've been around enough to recognize the signs, but the trouble is, I've never been around anyone like you! You don't run across many idealistic young girls just growing into womanhood in the circles I move in." He gave a short, bitter laugh. "I guess you just threw me, honey. It was a whole new ballgame, and I panicked." He turned toward the girl, looking deeply into her clear, green eyes. "I don't know where we go from here. I honestly don't."

There was nothing Kendrik could say. She was completely out of her depth, floundering around in an emotional sea.

Marcus reached for her hand, looking down at the long, slender, pink-tipped fingers. As he slowly traced the outline of each one with his own, he spoke again, not looking up. "If only you were older, someone like Erma." She flinched. "Then it wouldn't matter so much. I couldn't bear to see you suffer as my mother suffered. She was such a gentle person, really. In spite of all the everlasting wrangling, all she wanted was the security of a home and a family. My father, well, I guess I'm more like he was. I get restless after a while and have to keep moving on. I don't know—maybe I'm running from something."

Kendrik spoke now. "Or maybe you're searching for something."

"You may be right . . . you may be right." He sighed and stood up. "Let's get you home before I'm tempted to grab you again."

"For shaking or for loving?" she asked with a tremulous smile.

"Your guess is as good as mine. Anyhow, it's been an emotional hurricane, as usual, and we both need to get some rest before we fall apart. How'd you get here, anyhow? I didn't see your car."

She folded the lap robe and replaced it on the back of the sofa. "I parked in the back. I really came after the trunk and box."

Marcus threw back his head and roared with laughter. "Oh, Lord! I'm beginning to think that trunk has a spell on it!"

Kendrik grinned up at him as he opened the back door. "Do you think maybe Grandy's trying to put something over on us?"

They stepped out on the back porch. A streak of silver-gray light lay along the horizon just above the mirrorlike surface of the sound. Both stood silently for a moment in the chill thrall of a calm January daybreak. It was an overwhelmingly peaceful feeling that poured like a balm on the two of them.

"Can you manage all right?" He spoke quietly. "Aside from the fact that I'm dead tired—you aren't exactly the most restful person I know." He grinned down at her. "I've compromised you enough already without driving you home in the dawn's early light."

"I'll be fine," she assured him, and on impulse, she reached up and kissed his mouth lightly before hurrying to her car.

CHAPTER THIRTEEN

It was almost four o'clock before Kendrik struggled awake from the almost druglike sleep of utter exhaustion. The thorough chilling of the night before and the tremendous emotional expenditure had brought on a cold. She stood in front of the bathroom mirror, grimacing at the soreness of her throat and the throbbing in her head. A less beautiful girl would have looked awful. Kendrik merely succeeded in looking miserable.

She poured herself a glass of orange juice and shuddered as its acidity burned her throat. Pushing it aside, she sat and let her mind play over the events of the previous night.

In the gray light of another rainy afternoon, it seemed unreal, like a half-forgotten dream. Marcus. She spoke his name aloud as in her mind's eye she saw the tall, bronzed man, navy blue knit pullover stretched tightly across his broad shoulders, trim, navy slacks scarcely concealing the powerful muscles of his thighs, and the dark gleam of handsewn casual shoes.

The random thought passed through her mind that that was the first time she had seen him dressed in any other way than the usual island garb of denim and khaki.

Not for the first time, she wondered what his life was really like when he was not here in this insular village.

The sound of a car pulling up close to the porch interrupted her reverie, and she hastily ran her fingers through her touseled hair. Pulling on her old dark-green flannel robe she went to the door. She recognized the ancient green coupe of Mrs. O'Neal's that Vonnie sometimes drove.

As she held the door open for the scurrying dripping girl, Kendrik sneezed.

"Bless you!" said Vonnie. She took off her outer garments, and together they went into the other room. "You look terrible! What on earth have you been doing to yourself?" the dark-haired girl demanded. "Mama said you'd been over to Marcus's yesterday afternoon after those things of yours. You didn't stay long, did you?" There was an odd expression on Vonnie's face.

As much as she tried not to, Kendrik blushed. She turned toward the kitchen and busied herself with putting the kettle on to boil. "Which would you rather have, Vonnie, coffee or tea?" she asked. Her voice by now was beginning to thicken.

"You've got a cold, haven't you, honey? Did you get wet? Have you been out in this mess today?" Vonnie looked searchingly at her red-nosed friend.

Kendrik gave a short, husky laugh. "No . . . I guess I just got chilled somehow. I'll be okay as long as I can hole up here alone"—she stressed the last word—"and recover in my own sweet time."

"If you want me to go, just say so—not that I'd leave with you looking like this! At least, not before I see you settled in bed with some aspirin and hot lemonade with soda. Rest is the only thing that will really fix you up."

Kendrik poured two mugs of steaming coffee, adding cream and honey. "I'm not really sleepy. As a matter of fact, I just crawled out of bed!" For some peculiar reason, she wished she hadn't revealed that fact.

Changing the subject abruptly, Vonnie said, "I hear Marcus is back. Buck said he was down at the docks this morning, early. He must have come in on the first ferry." Getting no response from her friend, she plunked down her coffee mug and stood up. "Look, you're not fit company for man nor beast! Finish your coffee and let me fix you some hot soda lemonade. Come on, back into bed." Vonnie went into the bathroom and came back with the aspirin bottle, then busied herself in the kitchen while Kendrik crawled back under the covers.

As her mind struggled back to the surface of awareness, Kendrik dimly recalled having roused several times during the night. For some reason she seemed compelled to get up now, though she couldn't quite think why.

"Kendrik! Are you in there? Answer me!" That was why! Someone was beating on the door and calling out. Buck's voice came again, a note of anxiety reaching Kendrik's ear as she hastily shrugged into the green flannel robe.

"Wait a minute, wait a minute! Don't beat the door down!" She opened it to admit Buck Hollis, his perennially sunburned face showing concern.

"Boy! You must have been out like a light! I've been pounding on that door till my fists were sore!" He laughed down at his weather-hardened hands.

"I'm sorry, Buck, I have a cold and—come to think of it, I seem to have lost it somewhere along the way." She cleared her throat experimentally. "Vonnie dosed me up with her favorite panacea and tucked me in this morning, or was it last night? I seem to have lost all track of time, what with sleeping the clock around."

Buck, not a frequent visitor to the cottage, and never without Vonnie, seemed a little ill at ease.

"You'll have to give me a minute to wake up. Want a cup of coffee?" she said as her mind began to turn over possible excuses for his visit.

"I can't stay. I just stopped by to give you a message. Marcus said to tell you he's gone to the mainland, and he'll be coming in on the last ferry, and he's coming by to see you as soon as he gets in." The words came out in a rush as Buck edged toward the door. Though perfectly at ease in any nautical situation, the young man was painfully shy and awkward in most social settings.

"Well, thanks, Buck. I can't imagine why he's coming to see me." What a stupid thing to say! She felt a hot tide flow up to her cheeks.

Buck leaned around the door, grinned at her, and was gone.

For a long time, Kendrik simply sat with a complacent smile on her face, letting the thoughts ebb and flow through her mind. She reflected on the vagaries of the message system in a place without home telephones. For some reason, the idea of a man like Marcus having to send messages by someone else tickled her. It was reminiscent of the note-passing and whispered pass-it-on confidences common to schoolchildren.

She stood up and stretched her arms above her head. She felt completely restored—better, in fact, than she had in months! She didn't shy away from the reason, either. Marcus.

He was back, he had kissed her warmly. Oh, they had quarreled, yes—or rather, he had poured out his anger on her. All that was pushed to the back of her mind by the memory of those few minutes of tenderness, of unbelievable warmth and gentleness. She sighed, a beatific look on her face.

All of a sudden, she was spurred into action. Marcus was coming here to see her! If he came directly from the ferry as Buck had indicated, he should be here about dinnertime.

The next several hours sped by in a frenzy of activity. The cottage was cleaned and polished to within an inch of its life. Lacking the final touch of flowers, Kendrik hurried through the woods, followed by a reluctant Charlie, and gathered leaves, pine cones, bayberry, and cattails. These, combined with the sea oats she already had, made a handsome centerpiece for the round table.

She searched through her dresses—not that many, really—until she came to a long, dark green wool with a high neck and sleeves that hugged her arms only to flare out below the elbow.

"Yes!" She spoke aloud and hung the dress carefully on the door, then hurried to the kitchen to begin preparations for a dinner for two. Oyster cocktails, baked fish—the flounder she had in the refrigerator, surrounded by onions and potatoes and topped with strips of bacon would be delicious! What else? Tossed salad and fruit? Yes, her own special salad dressing and mixed fruit folded into madiera-flavored sour cream.

Fortunately, she had all the ingredients, and it was not long before she had the cocktails, the fruit cups, and the salad, covered by damp paper towels, stashed away in the refrigerator. She readied the fish, delighting in its appearance in her soft-blue glazed pottery baking dish, popped it into the oven to bake, and dashed to the bathroom for a shampoo and shower.

A satisfying sizzle and a delectable aroma issued from the warm little kitchen when she opened the bathroom door and stepped out. Standing in front of the dim old speckled mirror in her bedroom, she surveyed the picture before her. "Not bad, not bad," she told herself as she took in the still-damp tendrils curling around her dewy, bath-flushed face. She sat down in her long green-and-yellow flowered slip and reached for her hairbrush.

When she stepped back some time later, she gave her final approval to her own image in the dark green, simply styled dress that flowed over the curves of her body until it swirled out in a froth of fullness around her slender ankles. Sun-streaked gold-brown hair was smoothed into a knot at the back of her neck, the effect softened by the wispy, curling tendrils that escaped to caress her face.

Happiness brought a flush to her cheeks and a sparkle to her clear green eyes. Even the faint violet shadows, the result of her recent cold and of too many restless nights, added to the picture. She bit her naturally red lips, added a whiff of perfume, and hurried to the kitchen.

As she finished the last-minute preparations and sat down to catch her breath, an intimidating thought entered her mind: What if Marcus was only stopping by for a minute? What if he had no notion of dining here, of spending the evening with her? Embarrassment flooded through her, and she cringed, feeling like a perfect fool! She actually stood and took a quick step in the direction of the bedroom, thinking to change hurriedly into her old familiar jeans, but it was too late. Marcus was knocking at the door.

"Hello," she greeted him, still slightly abashed. "Come in. Buck said you were coming by for a minute, and I thought...if you haven't already had dinner, that is...I..." Her voice was constrained as she looked up at him, so vital, his very bulk in the heavy sheepskin jacket seeming to fill the small room.

"Hello, Kendrik." Something about his smile almost immobilized her for a moment. "I hoped you'd ask me, seeing there's not a single restaurant open on the island this time of year, and my cooking is strictly the breakfast variety!" He took off his coat, revealing a brown, silky knit shirt and tan pants that fit his lean, muscular body with an ease that bespoke hand tailoring.

"Buck said you'd been to the mainland. Business?" She could have swallowed her words. He would think she was prying into his affairs, and she was determined to keep this evening on a light and friendly basis. Too many of their meetings resulted in bitter verbal battles. Changing the subject back to food, she said, "As a matter of fact, I have a baked flounder in the oven, and you'd be doing me a favor if you'd help me finish it. I mean, I never feed fish scraps to Charlie on account of the bones. Sit down and I'll pour you a drink. That is, if you'll have either bourbon or madeira. I don't keep a very distinguished liquor supply, I'm afraid."

The evening floated by in a warm glow of good food and harmonious feelings. Marcus was highly complimentary of Kendrik's culinary ability, and she hugged to herself his obvious admiration for the way she looked tonight. She had been aware of his eyes following her as she moved around the room serving dinner and coffee afterward.

They had been sitting side by side on the sofa talking for some time, their subjects ranging from her father's absorption with history and her mother's with painting, to his late grandmother's idiosyncrasies. She had pried from him the information that he had degrees in both journalism and ornithology, and she assumed that he used his writing to support his interest in endangered species of birds.

For no reason at all, there was a pause in the conversation. One of those strange, ringing silences that sometimes occur.

"I've always heard that when it's quiet like this, a truly hushed feeling, that it's always either twenty minutes before the hour or twenty minutes after." She laughed, the soft, throaty sound doing little to relieve the odd feeling of tension that had suddenly sprung up between them.

"Kendrik, will you marry me?" The words hung in the air between them as if written there by a skywriter.

"Wha-a-at? Marcus?" She was stunned. "Oh, Marcus!

Yes!" She laughed through the tears that suddenly dimmed her eyes.

Marcus reached out one finger and placed it beneath her chin, turning her face to the lamplight and looking deeply, searchingly, into her eyes.

"Soon, darling... soon." He drew her to him in a close embrace, his arms protective and gentle as they cradled her. After a while, she raised her face to his, and she sensed the muffled thunder of his pulse as his lips slowly lowered to her own.

CHAPTER FOURTEEN

The frenzy of activities that took place during the succeeding days left her no time for second thoughts, had Kendrik been so inclined.

Marcus had returned to the mainland the next day, explaining that he could expedite matters so that when she joined him there would be only the slightest delay. He also asked Kendrik's permission to call her father and inform him of their plans, letting him know that a letter from Kendrik would follow in a few days.

Closing the cottage for an indefinite period and arranging for Charlie to stay first with the Hollises and then with the O'Neals kept her occupied at first. There was a regular checklist of duties for opening and shutting down the cottage that Grandy had prepared for the guidance of renters in the days when part of his income had derived from renting the place to hunters and fishermen. Before that, there were her clothes to pack up, some to be taken to Marcus's home after they returned and some to go with her.

As her list of chores left to do grew shorter, she became conscious of deliberately avoiding certain aspects of their relationship. There were doors that remained closed, and she made no effort to open them.

For some reason, Marcus was adamantly opposed to a church wedding. He insisted on the briefest possible ceremony in the little county seat on the mainland. Considering his previously expressed views on marriage, Kendrik quietly relinquished her ideas of a white wedding in the sturdy little Protestant church where her mother and father had been married.

Irregular ferry service during the stormiest part of the

year, lack of accommodations, traveling difficulties ... all these she put forth to herself as reasons to go along with Marcus's arrangements. Only in the last few minutes at night before sleep claimed her, when her defenses were at their lowest, did she listen to the tiny voice that questioned the haste, the lack of romance, the almost businesslike deliberation that marked the preparations for her marriage.

She felt strangely like a tightrope walker, aware of being supported by some strong but wavering filament, too uneasy to look down and examine it closely, daring only to put one foot before the other in the prescribed manner.

Vonnie and her mother crossed the inlet with Kendrik, and they were "headed down the final lap," according to the exuberantly chattering young nurse.

They arrived in town late in the evening, and Kendrik tried hard to hide her disappointment at not finding Marcus waiting for her in the town's only hotel. The message left for her at the desk read simply, "Have gone to Norfolk to bring back special wedding guests. Meet me at the courthouse at ten. Marcus." No Love, no Dearest ... just Marcus. She slept little that night.

After meeting a tender, solicitous, but somehow impersonal Marcus the next morning for the legal requirements, Kendrik was glad she had arranged to go shopping with the O'Neals. It seemed that Marcus had several business details to attend to before he could be free for a short trip, so after a rather hasty lunch, they parted until time for the ceremony.

"Here goes my life's savings," Kendrik laughed later on to Vonnie. "I never dreamed I'd be spending it for a trousseau!"

The small town boasted few shops of any quality, but fortunately, they had to look no farther than the first one before finding the perfect wedding dress. It was of sheer wool crepe, the color of apricots. The low, rounded neckline was draped softly with a cowl and the bias-cut fabric fell to a graceful mid-calf lenght after clinging lovingly to her slight, rounded figure. Brown suede shoes and bag and a matching bandeau for her hair completed the ensemble, and Kendrik was delighted with her luck in finding them.

Vonnie insisted on helping her buy lingerie, though Kendrik protested that she already had enough.

"This is different," Vonnie laughed. "You don't want to upset tradition by wearing underwear instead of lingerie, do you?"

Kendrik colored under the gentle teasing of her friend. But she agreed to buy something frilly.

"Just look at this," said Nina O'Neal, holding up a transparent, lacy confection. "Just look at that delicate embroidery. Here, Kendrik, you have to have this one!"

Kendrik had a little over two hours before time to get dressed for the small ceremony. Afterward, they planned to get together back at the hotel with Marcus's best man and the Harrises, an older couple he had described to her over lunch as "family."

There had been no time for Kendrik to meet them last night, as they had arrived with Marcus long after she had gone to bed. Evelyn Harris, he had explained, was his only real relative, his mother's cousin. She and her husband, Hal, had been involved in a serious automobile accident just over a year ago, and as a result, neither of them drove anymore.

"I hated like hell not to be here when you arrived, Kendrik. But I especially wanted them to meet you, and it seemed the only way to get them here. Mike's going to be late," he had explained. "Even the *owner* of the newspaper chain has certain deadlines, and anyway, I can't see Evelyn and Hal jammed into Mike's little TR-6, racing against time to get here."

The excited fluttering of Vonnie and her mother did nothing to help Kendrik to get ready. As they rushed around the cluttered hotel room, getting into each other's way and laughing uproariously, Kendrik sighed and sank down deeper into the tub of warm suds. Against the muffled murmurings from the next room, her thoughts ranged over the past few days.

Impossible to think that such changes could be wrought in so short a time. Who was this tall, strange man with the compelling blue eyes? Was this odd harmony, this dangerous affinity that could charge the atmosphere between them almost enough to produce its own lightning, enough to base a marriage on? What could she possibly have been thinking of when she agreed to marry him? How could she even consider putting the rest of her life in his hands, those strong brown hands that had shaken her and caressed her? What could a man like Marcus want with a naive, gauche schoolgirl like herself? Child, he had called her. And, in so many ways, that was exactly what she was.

She was struck by a sudden chilling thought: What if he hadn't really meant it when he asked her to marry him? What if he already regretted it? In one corner of her mind she heard the echo of something he had once said, "It was a mistake I don't intend to repeat," and he had been talking of marriage. He had never actually told her he loved her. Did she love him enough to make up for the lack of love on his part? And could she make him forget Erma? And all the others?

"Hurry, Kendrik!" Vonnie called. "Your things are all laid out. We have to be downstairs in twenty-five minutes, so if you need us, we'll be in the next room getting dressed."

CHAPTER FIFTEEN

For such a small building, the courthouse had a surprising amount of dignity. The miniature row of steps leading up to the porticoed entrance of the old brick building seemed most impressive to Kendrik as she stood between the two O'Neal women. They proceeded up the steps rather slowly, in deference to Nina O'Neal's hip. It had held up remarkably well under the whirlwind of activity.

As she stepped into the high-ceilinged vestibule, Kendrik felt very young, very small, and very alone. Then she saw Marcus. He stood before her looking rather unlike himself in his dark blue, beautifully tailored suit with his gray silk tie. Only his eyes, those deep, clear, blue eyes, reassured her. As he looked directly at her, the surroundings seemed to fade away, and there was only Marcus . . . only the two of them, Marcus and Kendrik. He held out his hand, and she moved toward him.

"Are you ready?" he asked softly.

"I'm ready," she breathed.

Sounds of laughter, of congratulations and best wishes burst on her consciousness as she and Marcus turned, hand in hand, and faced the barrage of confetti and rice.

Clinging to the warm, strong hand of her husband as if it were a lifeline, she beamed at all her dear friends. People she had not yet met, many of them, nevertheless, her dear, dear friends. Through a haze of euphoria she saw Mrs. O'Neal weeping openly. Vonnie, looking lovely in a new suit of teal blue, was clinging to Buck's hand. She had not even known Buck was there. A tall, white-haired woman whose lined face was still beautiful stood smiling at her warmly. Kendrik moved toward her swiftly and clasped the extended hand.

"You must be Evelyn Harris. Thank you, thank you so much for coming." She turned to the tall, completely bald man beside her whose eyes sparkled under surprisingly dark brows. "And you're Hal Harris, aren't you? I'm Kendrik Haynes—no, I'm not!" She joined in the laughter and felt Marcus's arm close around her shoulder.

"Meet my wife, Kendrik Haynes Manning. Ken, these are my closest friends and my only family, Evelyn and Hal. And this"—turning to a ruggedly attractive man with iron gray hair and matching eyes—"is Mike. By the look on his face, it's a good thing I saw you first!"

Mike Stevens laughed and took her hand in a crushing grip. "Right the first time, old man, and I'll just lay claim to my reward for standing beside you while you sealed your doom." He put both arms around Kendrik and pulled her close as he proceeded to kiss her soundly. "There," he said to Marcus, dusting his hands together, "that'll give you something to live up to!"

"May I kiss the groom?" came a husky, familiar voice, and Kendrik spun around to see Erma O'Neal, lovelier than ever in violet wool and rich, dark mink, hooking an arm through Marcus's and raising her full, red lips for a kiss, which he laughingly bestowed.

An ice-cold finger touched her heart for an instant as Kendrik forced a smile to her face. "I didn't see you, Erma. I didn't really see anybody, I guess." She attempted a smile that didn't quite come off.

"Oh, I couldn't let Mike make the trip all alone. Besides, I knew Marcus would want his dearest . . . friends to be here." Her eyes glittered with a feeling that Kendrik was sure didn't match the smile that came with practiced ease.

"Come on, darling, champagne and a chance to get acquainted with all these people before we leave." Marcus drew Kendrik close to his side, and they left the courthouse together.

For such a small gathering, the party in the funny little hotel lounge was remarkably lively. The odd assortment of furniture that had somehow found its way into the town's only hotel in the seventy-odd years since it had been established reflected expediency as well as the wildly divergent tastes of the several owners over the years. It seemed that nothing had been removed, but only added to, and it was against this background that Kendrik found herself thoroughly enjoying Evelyn Harris's accounts of a young Marcus as he went through the various stages of development leading to the mature, highly successful man he was today.

"He's always been extremely popular. Of course, his looks and personality alone would ensure that." As she took a sip of champagne, Kendrik wondered fleetingly at the phraseology.

"Still, there's always been something . . . almost aloof, a sort of reserve, even when he was at his wildest. And he was wild, I'll assure you!" Evelyn Harris looked beyond the confines of the room, into a time she held in her memories. "It was almost as if he were driven to see just how far he could go. I never really got beneath his guard. I'm sure no one did." Her attention came back to the tender young woman before her. "Before you, my dear. I can't tell you how glad I am that Marcus has chosen so wisely. You're right for him. You're a giver, and all the others have been takers."

Kendrik couldn't have found a reply even if she had had time, but at that instant, Marcus had touched her gently on the neck and informed her that they must be leaving within a few minutes if they were to make their airline connections in Norfolk. He had told her earlier that they were to board a plane shortly before midnight, but other than letting her know in plenty of time that she would be needing beach clothes, he had still not let her in on their final destination.

"Everything's ready, Marcus. I saw the porter get the bags about fifteen minutes ago, but if there's time, I'd like to run up to the room to freshen up before we go."

Kendrik was just drying her hands in the bathroom when she heard the outer door open and close. Thinking Vonnie had come up to speak to her before she left, she called out through the partially closed connecting door, "Oh, Vonnie, wasn't it marvelous? Can you believe I'm really married? Mrs. Marcus Manning! I'm dreaming!" She stepped through the doorway, still talking, and halted suddenly as she came face to face with Erma O'Neal.

Gone was Erma's mask of polite goodwill. Open malice glittered in her eyes as she spoke.

"You're a lot smarter than I gave you credit for! Who would have thought that you'd have the nerve to try that stunt?" She gave a short, vicious laugh that chilled Kendrik to the bones. "Well, it worked! He's well and truly caught in your nasty little trap! You can imagine how he was feeling when he came to my apartment to tell me about it! All our plans down the drain, and all because some cheap little sneak had the nerve to hide in his bedroom and get herself seen by Buck and all the fishermen, leaving early the next morning! Well, congratulations! You'll need it! Now we'll see how you like living with a man who despises you, a man who'll always be thinking of another woman whenever he makes love to you!"

From a thousand miles away came the sound of the

door being slammed. It registered only dimly on the rigid figure in the middle of the impersonal hotel room. The eyes in the wretched, ashen face looked like two enormous bruises. She had no conception of the passing time as she stood, swaying slightly on icy feet.

Something rapped sharply on the door. It opened as someone said, "Hurry, sweet, we've got to rush. Aren't you ready yet?" Marcus stopped still as he saw her face. "Kendrik! What's wrong? Are you ill?" He stepped to her side almost instantly and grasped her shoulders in a bruising hold. "What is it, darling? Come, lie on the bed while I get a doctor!"

"No, no . . . I'm all right." She returned from the frozen, mindless world that had held her in shock for an eon. "I . . . I . . . just felt faint for a moment. Too . . . too much excitement, champagne." She regained an almost unnatural sort of control and was able to assure Marcus that she was perfectly capable of going downstairs to say good-bye to all their well-wishers. Anything, rather than stay in this small, intimate room with the one man in the world she couldn't face now!

Shock, embarrassment, and a terrible sense of loss fought for dominance within her as she went through the motions of smiling, shaking hands, kissing cheeks, and murmuring the expected phrases—at least, she hoped they were the right words. Afterward she could remember not a thing of the leavetaking nor of the two-hour trip to the airport. The long day, the lateness of the hour, and the strain were excuses enough, and she pretended to sleep as her dazed mind tried to reassemble the shattered fragments of her situation.

Boarding the flight for Miami, Kendrik felt a small niggle of disappointment, ridiculous under the circumstances. Miami was not a place she thought she would particularly enjoy, and she had thought that Marcus would have chosen a place that was less... less Miami-like. Neither of them was the type to enjoy swimming pools and nightclubs.

But then, what do I know about him? she asked herself. At least in a place like Miami, he won't have to spend much time alone with me. Erma's words returned to twist a knife in her again. All I really know about him is that he's chivalrous enough to sacrifice his own happiness to protect the reputation of a stupid girl! What am I going to do? she wept inwardly.

Inside Miami International Airport, Kendrik had the feeling of unreality that comes from being in a strange place among strange people at a time of night when one should be asleep. Added to the sense of displacement was the companionship of this tall, strange man who held her arm and hurried her across the terazzo floor to the Mexican Airline desk, where he produced two visitors' cards and tickets before hustling her through the corridor to the loading airliner.

Only when they were being settled into their seats by a beautiful dark-skinned stewardess with a captivating accent did she turn to Marcus for enlightenment.

His grimness made way for a slight smile, the first in some time, as he answered the question put to him.

"Cozumel, a small island off the Yucatan peninsula. I haven't been there before, but friends of mine described it to me, and it sounded like a place we'd both enjoy."

He bit back the remainder of his thoughts, that he had looked forward to their sharing the first visit to a place that was new to them both. He had no idea what had happened to change things so drastically, but the pale, quiet woman beside him bore little resemblance to the glowing, beautiful girl he had married. Only the fact that they hadn't had a single moment alone since boarding the plane in Norfolk had kept him from trying to reach the bottom of the mystery.

Kendrik had slept almost all of the flight from Norfolk to Miami. It was as though an overload switch somewhere in her mind had tripped out rather than blow a fuse, and now that they were once more settled in the hushed atmosphere of a dimly lighted, droning, pressurized cabin, her eyelids began to flutter down once again.

Just before sleep claimed her, she mumbled a soft "Thank you," to Marcus. She was not quite sure what it was for, but she felt such concern, such chivalry as he had shown deserved some recognition. In her sleep-dazed condition, she was aware of a tremendous surge of emotion toward the man sitting so quietly in the shadows beside her, but gratitude was the only feeling she could pick out and identify at the moment.

It was still fairly early in the morning when Kendrik and Marcus walked from the small jetliner into the airport at Cozumel and, shortly afterward, out to the Volkswagen jeep they had hired for their stay.

She had a fleeting impression of blinding sunlight, of voluptuous tropical flowers, and contrasting sharply, lined up outside the airport, a row of tattered and dilapidated World-War-Two fighter planes. She blinked her eyes, thinking it a delusion, but there they remained, the propellers, as often as not, resting on the ground nearby or completely missing.

The paved road, marred only occasionally by potholes, led past an unbelievable sea. It was Kendrik's first look at the Caribbean, and she was totally unprepared for the jewellike clarity and the myriad shades of blue.

After two or three miles, they stopped by a hedge of

oleander and hibiscus that surrounded a large white stucco building. Because of the hedge and the towering palm trees, Kendrik was unable to gain any idea of the size and shape of the structure, but she surmised it was a hotel as Marcus jumped out and was met almost at once by a white-coated, dark-skinned man.

They were led through a series of walkways to a door that opened directly onto the beach, only a few yards from the crystalline waters of the sea. The smiling young Mexican who placed their luggage beside the door murmured, *"Gracias, senor,"* and disappeared.

There had scarcely been a dozen words exchanged by the two people, facing each other, since they had set foot on this exotic, exclusive little island. As they stood, one on each side of the louvered door, searching each other's eyes for a clue as to how to proceed, Marcus was aware of the deep violet shadows that smudged the transparent skin around her clouded green eyes. The look of weariness added a fragility that smote him, and he moved toward her, smiling with great tenderness as he placed a hand on each side of her face. Despite the understanding smile, his eyes revealed very little of his emotions as he spoke softly.

"You're tired, Kendrik. We're both out on our feet, I expect. What's needed is a long sleep all in one place before we . . . do any talking. A thousand miles or more in one swoop is a bit much!" He was aware of the delicacy of her cheekbones beneath the cool, smooth flesh as he leaned down and touched first one eyelid, then the other with his lips. "You use the bathroom first, if you want to. I'll put the bags in the other room, and then I'm going out for a few minutes to find some cigarettes. Back in fifteen or twenty minutes."

After Marcus left the room, Kendrik looked around in a state not far removed from panic. What was she doing in this strange hotel on an island where they didn't speak her language, nor she theirs... and with a complete stranger? A stranger who had only married her from a sense of pity, duty!

The love she had felt for Marcus was lost somewhere in the confusion of emotions that stormed her frail body. Breathing deeply to still the frightened soul fluttering like a captive bird within the exhausted body, she went to the door and looked into the bedroom. Two double beds, two bedside tables, two dressers, two chairs... and one pile of luggage. She returned to the token living room, which consisted of a bamboo settee, a coffee table, and a gaily cushioned chair. She picked up a coral-colored blossom that had fallen from the bouquet on the low coffee table and stood shredding it, unthinkingly, as her eyes moved beyond the louvered windows to the travel-poster scene outdoors.

Get a grip on yourself! Marcus is not a beast, she thought. "The only way to handle the situation is to accept the fact that Marcus married me out of respect," she whispered to herself. Respect for Grandy, for the Haynes name on the banks, where it's been an honorable name for almost three hundred years, and for his own reputation, which wouldn't be helped by rumors of a sordid little affair with a young nobody!

Moving swiftly to the bedroom she opened her big leather suitcase, a heavy relic of the pre-vinyl days. She drew out a sheer chiffon nightgown, the delicate color of eggshells. Laughing rather bitterly, she told herself she should have brought the old white flannel.

When Marcus returned a little while later, there was a drift of steam from the bathroom, indicating its recent occupation, but Kendrik was asleep in one of the big beds, her face to the wall.

"Kendrik? Are you awake?" he asked softly, not expecting an answer. The slight mound beneath the white bedspread seemed to become even more rigid, the sound of soft breathing stilled for a moment. He sighed and turned away.

CHAPTER SIXTEEN

The light in the bedroom was a dim, dark green as it filtered through the junglelike growth outside the two small windows. Kendrik sat up and looked swiftly at the bed on the other side of the room. Empty. She showered quickly and slipped into a cool white shift, moving to the living-room windows as she brushed her silky hair into a semblance of order and tied it back with a turquoise scarf.

Through the wide, louvered windows, she saw several people: a Mexican couple sitting on a rock watching their baby play in the shallows, several masked and snorkled figures of indeterminate age cavorting farther out, and three people sitting in the colorful wooden lounge chairs placed by the management along the beach.

The woman was exquisite in a dramatic way, her blue-black hair contrasting sharply with a parchment white skin. Her only note of color was a brilliant red mouth, for she was clad, startlingly enough, in solid black. She seemed engrossed in a conversation with Marcus—a Marcus looking more magnetically attractive than ever in his white slacks and navy blue knit top.

Sitting on the other side of the woman in black was a middle-aged man wearing faded bathing trunks, a lurid sport shirt, and bedroom slippers! He was reading a paper from the bulging briefcase beside him and paid no attention to the two people beside him, who were so engrossed in conversation.

Kendrik hesitated for a moment, reluctant to interrupt Marcus and the strange woman. Then, prompted by a sudden surge of hunger, she picked up a floppy, wide-brimmed white hat and went outside.

Marcus saw her as soon as she left the door, almost as if

he had been watching for her. He stood and smiled a welcome, extending his hand to her. Drawing her to his side, he turned to the other two. "I'd like you to meet my wife, Kendrik. Dear, these are the Kleins."

"Fred and Mara, please. I can't abide formality at the beach. It seems so out of context." Mara Klein smiled as she touched fingers briefly with Kendrik. At closer range, she appeared a little older than Kendrik had first thought, the tiny wrinkles that penalize thin, fine-grained skin having entrenched themselves on her lovely face. Her smile seemed genuinely welcoming, and Kendrik responded before turning toward Fred Klein.

There was something almost endearing about the man, in spite of—or maybe because of—his odd attire. Perhaps it had to do with the horn-rimmed glasses sliding down his bulbous nose, or the pipe ashes that slid from his lap as he stood. It was not diminished by his firm voice nor the incisive glance as he transferred his clutter of papers to the other hand and clasped hers in a warm, firm grip. "Hmmm. Well, little lady...mean to tell me you're married to this jack-of-all-trades? Why, the last time I saw this old pirate, he was cutting a mean swathe through a pretty little bunch of...er...ah..."

"Fred, Kendrik and Marcus haven't had lunch yet, and the dining room won't be open much longer." Mara turned to them. "Shall we see you later?"

"At dinner tonight. Join us." Marcus waved a casual hand as he guided Kendrik in the direction of the glass-fronted dining room. "We can eat out here, but I rather think it's too sunny at the moment, don't you? Let's go inside."

By unspoken mutual consent, they waited until the soft-spoken young waiter took their order in his strongly accented English. He filled their goblets with cold bottled water and discreetly disappeared.

"Did you know the Kleins before we came here?"

"Yes. As a matter of fact, Fred is the one who told me about this place. He's a public relations director for a large intercontinental corporation, and when they're not traveling, they spend a lot of time here, although I didn't know they'd be here now."

"She's beautiful. I think I like her quite a bit, even if her sophistication does scare me a little. And he's a teddy bear."

Marcus threw back his head and roared. "Oh, honey! I doubt if Frederick F. Klein has ever been called a teddy bear before in his life! He's been called a lot of things, and not all of them very flattering, but not that! Besides being public relations director and one of the major stockholders, he's something of a financial wizard, too."

Shaking his head and still laughing softly, Marcus went on. "Mara is great! She was a ballet dancer with one of the better-known troupes. I got to know her while I was messing around with television a while back. Anyhow, Fred had been wanting to marry her for so long, and all of a sudden, she capitulated. I think it stunned him! She doesn't seem to regret it at all, giving up dancing."

They finished the clear broth, deftly flavored by a slice of thin lime.

"Do they know...that is, have you told them that we...?"

"No, Kendrik. I haven't seen them in almost a year, so there's no way they can know how long we've been married."

"Well, do you mind if we, ah, let them think—"

"Of course. Kendrik, don't worry so. It'll be all right. This is not the proper time to talk about it, but you and I have some things to hash out. Until we do, just trust me."

As she applied herself to a concoction of mixed seafood in a subtle sauce of some kind, a fragment of conversation from the past ran through her mind. It was a whole new ballgame. Marcus had said that about her not long ago. Well, it's a new ballgame for me, too, so maybe we can learn the rules together.

Stepping out on the patio after lunch, Kendrik caught sight of a boat pulling alongside the concrete pier in front of their hotel. "What gorgeous lines," she observed. "It looks almost as if it had been a schooner, or some other type of sailing vessel. What's it doing here, Marcus? Do you know?" She was moving swiftly across the palm-shaded sand to the pier where the vessel was making fast.

"That must be the San Francisco thing. I'll check into it if you'd like me to."

"Oh, would you? What San Francisco thing? Could we go aboard, do you think?" She was tugging at his hand without thinking, in an effort to hurry him along through the throng of sunburned people disembarking.

Kendrik stopped midway along the angled concrete pier in admiration of the graceful lines of the thirty-five-foot craft. From her vantage point, she could see its obvious age under the coat of spanking white paint. It occurred to her as she noted the ultramarine blue, the rose red, and mustard-colored trim and interior that those same colors on any boat at home would be garish. Here in the Caribbean, where everything took on a technicolor brilliance, the flamboyant boats were like jungle birds in their element.

Marcus rejoined her. "It's on for tomorrow. We'll leave here early in the morning and go for about an hour's run down the coast to San Francisco beach. Along the way there'll be diving over a coral reef that's supposed to be

something special. The crew members will catch fish and
conch, and later on they'll cook it for our lunch while we
swim and explore the beach at San Francisco."

"Oh, Marcus, that sounds marvelous! I wish it were
already tormorrow!" She could have bitten her tongue.

"We'll try to think of some way to speed the time," he
replied in a noncommittal sort of tone.

"Hi, you two! We're going to town. Want to come?"
Mara Klein waved from the shore. She had changed her
black pantsuit for a full-skirted sheer black cotton, and
despite the long sleeves and the wide-brimmed black hat,
she somehow managed to look cool and casual.

Marcus queried Kendrik with a raised eyebrow, his
hand under her arm as they walked toward the waiting
woman.

"I didn't know there was a town," Kendrik said. "We
didn't come through it on the way from the airport, did
we, Marcus?"

"No, but I understand it's not far away. Small place,
shops for the tourists, that sort of thing."

Actually, San Miguel was a bit more than just shops for
the tourists, but it still retained a small-town feeling. Its
various shops with their pink, blue, lavender, and green
fronts, the riotous flowers tumbling over walls and fences,
and the proximity of the glittering, jewellike waters of the
Caribbean enchanted Kendrik as she and Marcus, along
with the Kleins, parked the rental car outside one of the
larger shops.

She and Mara went inside, leaving Fred and Marcus
examining a display of diving gear next door. Mara
quickly chose several dresses and disappeared into a
fitting room, and Kendrik moved over to a display of
native jewelry. She was discussing in her high-school
Spanish a pair of ornate golden earrings, fashioned to

resemble a Mayan figure, when Marcus entered. He reached her side and looked down at the trays of rings, bracelets, and earrings.

"Did you find anything you'd like?"

"Oh, they're all rather lovely. The gold ones are nice, but they're far too large."

"What about a ring?"

"Oh, Marcus... this has spoiled me for all other jewelry, I'm afraid." She held out her hand, displaying the old-fashioned pink-gold band set with opals and garnets that he had given her for a wedding band.

"It's not particularly valuable, I'm afraid, but my mother put it away for me in their safe-deposit box when I was about five, hoping, I suppose, that I'd give it to my bride someday." He looked vaguely uncomfortable as he turned away to the room where the dresses hung.

"Have you looked in here? Five will get you ten that's where Mara headed immediately."

"Yes, she found several things to try. I think they're rather expensive, though, and not my style at all." She laughed a little uncertainly. "Jeans are more my thing, you'll have to admit."

Marcus strolled over to a rack and pulled out a long, plain white wool whose only ornamentation was a wide band of self-embroidered openwork around the bottom. He held it up to her and squinted through a half-closed eye.

"Oh, Marcus, don't be silly!" She covered her embarrassment with an impatient tone of voice. "I have all the dresses I need, and that's far too expensive for me!"

"You'll oblige me by trying it on, Mrs. Manning." He stressed the name in a cool, impersonal manner and handed her the dress.

"Senora? This way please."

Kendrik followed the exquisite little dark-haired girl to the fitting room. Mara, slipping into an orange creation, hurried to meet her.

"Oh, good! I didn't know what you were in the market for, but a woman can always use another dress—and another and another!" She laughed like the sound of wind chimes as she pirouetted in the full, orange skirt.

"Oh, Mara, I don't know. Should I? I think Marcus wants to buy me a dress and—" She broke off, not knowing exactly what she wanted from the older woman; advice, encouragement, or simply a friend. It was just that simple. She desperately needed to talk with another woman, a friend who could listen, understand, and reassure her. Instinct told her that this woman, this exotic creature from such a different background, a different age, would understand all the misgivings and doubts that had hounded her since that awful moment she had learned the truth of her marriage from Erma. This was not the time, but if the occasion arose, it would be good to know she had someone to turn to.

"Try it on. You'll know if it's right; I won't have to tell you. Anyhow, Marcus will love having a doll like you to dress up. Underneath that rather tough exterior, he's always been a sensitive man, and he appreciates real beauty more than most any man I know."

"You know him so well, don't you, Mara?"

"Well enough to suspect that this husband business is new to him." Her smile relieved some of the tension Kendrik felt at her words. "Don't worry, child, if you want it kept under your hat, I won't let out a peep, but you'll have to stop looking at him the way you do. That child-peering-through-the-toystore-window look is a dead giveaway! And he's not much better!"

"What do you mean?" Kendrik spoke through layers of sheer white wool.

"Well, if you really want to know, he looks like—" She pursed her mouth and stepped back to get a better view of the golden-looking girl in white wool. "He looks as if he'd just been given a Faberge egg and hadn't the slightest idea what to do with it." She frowned slightly, considering her own words.

"What's the matter, didn't it come with a set of instructions?" Marcus's voice came through the curtains to the fitting area.

"Ta-daa." Mara made a stage entrance, arms flung wide, but after the briefest of glances, the man's eyes moved to the almost diffident girl behind her. Kendrik's pale gold skin and deeper gold hair glowed with an incandescence above the pure white gown that revealed even as it concealed the exquisite lines of her young body. Her clear green eyes looked straight at Marcus, and for the two of them, no one else existed for a moment.

"She must have it, Marcus, don't you agree? If Fred will indulge me one more time—and he will, if I know my Fred—we'll sport our new finery at dinner tonight, and afterward we'll listen to the band in the bar while we sip something cool and rum-filled." She turned to Kendrik. "There's a resident band with three members and they only know three songs, but since the rhythm never varies, you soon stop listening to the melody, and no one ever knows the difference."

The rest of the afternoon passed in a confusion of shops offering more or less the same fare. Marcus and Fred took refuge on one of the benches lining the waterfront, and Kendrik, conscious of the limited amount of money in her bag, was ready to go back to the hotel long before Mara tired of trying on the surprisingly chic dresses to be found in the little shops.

"I know I'm paying resort prices and I could find the same thing at home for a fraction, but Fred spends so much time reading those endless reports and I've sampled all the tourist treats this island has to offer. Rather awful of me, isn't it?" Mara grinned at Kendrik over her shoulder.

"Don't let her kid you, Kendrik. She wouldn't buy a dress for a hundred dollars if she could find the same dress somewhere else for a hundred and fifty!"

"Really, Fred! Why should I buy a hundred dollar dress when I can have a hundred-fifty one instead?"

Kendrik joined in the general laughter as they pulled up to the hotel. Her first day as a tourist—her mind balked at the term "honeymooner"—had left her rather limp.

"We'll see you both about nine in the dining om, all right?" Mara called over to them as she and Fred rned toward the lobby to go to their second-floor room.

CHAPTER SEVENTEEN

It was late when Kendrik and Marcus said goodnight to the Kleins outside the bar. Mara had declined the trip to San Francisco beach with them.

"Darlings, it appeals to my sense of the dramatic to keep my lily white complexion in the age of toasted bikini-clad belles. I'd much rather be known as the elegant creature with the porcelain skin than as that old gal with all the wrinkles! No, you run along and enjoy it. I'll stick around here and annoy Fred."

Fingering a wilted oleander blossom, Kendrik wandered toward the pier. She did not admit, even to herself, her reluctance to return to their room, but as Marcus followed her she pretended an intense interest in the tiny fish that swam beneath them in the spotlighted, crystal-clear water.

She smelled a drift of pipe tobacco on the spicy-sweet night air and turned, seeing her husband for a brief moment as a stranger might. His tall, white-jacketed form little resembled the Marcus she had first met on another island, another beach. For an instant she was able to see herself objectively, her unfamiliar chic a not-unacceptable foil for his urbane good looks. The image of the elegant, sophisticated couple alone in the wildly romantic setting wavered for a moment, then disappeared as Marcus spoke wryly from behind her back.

"D'you suppose Charlie would feel comfortable on a beach like this?"

She was wrenched back to normality, once more an ill-at-ease, newly married, small-town girl floundering around in an untenable situation.

"I don't know if one ocean smells like another or not.

It's a different world to me, but dogs don't go by the way a place looks, do they?" She wondered if Charlie missed her or if he was content in familiar territory with the O'Neals to feed him and speak to him occasionally.

"It's a different setting, Kendrik, not a different world. We're no different from the way we were up in your grandfather's attic, or in my office or your cottage. Remember?"

The cool night air did little to chill the flame that rose in her cheeks, and she moved away from him slightly. Oh, yes, Marcus, she thought, I remember. But you're wrong about one thing. There is a difference. We're married.

"It's late, Kendrik. You can't stay out here much longer." He took her arm and began to lead her rather reluctant body back the way they had come. One small light shone through the window of the suite as they approached the door, and it revealed the pallor of her face.

As the door closed behind them, she felt his hands on her shoulders, drawing her back against his warmth. "Kendrik, darling," he whispered against her hair, "it's been a strange time, hasn't it? Almost like seeing two players on a stage. But now—" He turned her in his arms and lowered his firm lips to hers. As though someone had flicked a switch and turned off the rest of the world, Kendrik's awareness began and ended in Marcus's arms. Her arms crept up around his neck, and her kiss spoke silently of all the love in her bewildered heart. It was all but impossible to deny this man anything he asked of her, loving him as she did—even knowing that she meant nothing more to him than . . . than what? Was it propinquity? Physical attraction? That, surely, and therein lay the danger. As the chill remembrance of Erma and her prior claim rushed over her, Kendrik drew away.

"No," she whispered in a strangled voice. "No."

They stood, frozen in a moment of silence, before Marcus turned, swearing softly under his breath, and slammed out into the night.

Hours later, as Kendrik lay rigid in her bed, eyes open to the darkness, she heard sounds of laughter and the insistent beat of Latin music coming from a distance.

Marcus still had not come in when she finally succumbed to exhaustion.

It seemed only minutes later that she felt herself being shaken and heard a voice saying, "C'mon, Kendrik. We have a boat to catch, remember?"

Kendrik sat up, her eyes still not focusing properly, and brushed the tangled hair from her face. Looking blankly into the expressionless face above her, it took her several seconds before she began to recall their parting the night before. Before she could register any degree of emotion of any sort, he was saying something about coffee in the other room as he turned away.

After a hasty shower, she slipped into a cool, buttonfront dress over her bathing suit. Steeling herself to face Marcus with at least a modicum of imperturbability, she opened the door to the other room, only to find it empty. Draperies had been opened to the soft, morning air, and she saw on the small table a tray of rolls and coffee, as well as the daily bouquet of fresh flowers.

She poured herself a cup of the rich-tasting brew and stood at the open window sipping it as she watched several small boys diving from the pier. All of them were brown as acorns, and as she watched them, one of the smallest turned in her direction, laughing. Above the square, white teeth were the bluest eyes she had ever seen—almost! A sudden pang smote her as she envisioned another boy about twenty-five years ago. Would he have been laughing and playing in the water, secure in the knowledge that his parents were watching?

At the same moment that Kendrik saw the jaunty little vessel breasting the ripples, Marcus called through the door.

"Hurry up, Ken. Grab a roll and bring your coffee."

They were immediately caught up in the small, excited group from the hotel that was boarding the *Celia* for the day's outing. She noted a few guests whom she had seen before, in the dining room, the bar, or on the beach, including a particularly vivacious brunette whose eyes had seemed to glow at Marcus wherever they went.

Marcus lifted Kendrik by the waist and swung her aboard the canopied deck, jumping down to stand beside her at the rail as they pulled away. He was as polite and casually friendly as if she were someone he had only recently met and in whom he had no particular interest.

Maybe he didn't, came the chilling thought. Make up your mind, she told herself. Isn't this what you wanted? No! From somewhere the feeling came to answer the thought. Not this distance, this cool politeness, this indifference.

"Do you dive?"

She looked at the young man standing beside her, puzzlement showing in her eyes.

"You know. Scuba. Snorkle." He grinned at Kendrik, and his attractive young face, covered with freckles under the untidy mop of brass-colored hair, betrayed his admiration for the slim, lightly tanned girl before him.

"You have that year-around-type tan that matches your hair and usually means skiing, sailing, and tennis. I thought perhaps a bit of diving, too, hmmm?"

"Would you believe clamming, fishing, and hanging the wash out on the line?" she laughed.

"Never! Princesses of the royal blood who spend winters in Cozumel wouldn't know the first thing about how to attach wet clothes to a clothesline. That's left for poor bachelor schoolteachers like me and pickle-faced old maids!" His glance strayed to her left hand, resting lightly on the rail. "I see by the hardware on the left hand that you're not a pickle-faced old maid. Pity...I was rather fancying myself in the role of gigolo to a desperate maiden lady." His exaggerated sigh brought forth a giggle.

"Come along, pickle-face." Marcus had silently returned to her side without her being aware. "Let's go forward and lie out on the deck."

As they settled down on the canvas sling chairs, Marcus with his shirt removed to bare his dark, matted chest to the sun, Kendrik felt like a gauche teenager caught in a foolish act. That's ridiculous, she told herself. She had been doing absolutely nothing for which she need be ashamed. After all, Marcus had walked away and left her, without a word, almost as soon as they pulled away from the pier.

"You seem to have a penchant for schoolteachers."

"What do you mean?"

"First Jess, then your brass-topped gigolo friend."

"I didn't realize you knew Jeff." Her mind raced back to the time when Jeff was a daily visitor, bringing the children to the cottage.

Marcus leaned over to unbutton her skirt, beginning at the hemline. "You'll miss this sun when we return. Don't waste it. I met Jeff a year or so ago. Very likable guy. Serious, dedicated, responsible—good husband material, don't you think?"

"Marcus, I . . . What do you want me to say? Yes, I know Jeff. I like him enormously. He's one of the finest men I've ever met, and perhaps, in different circumstances . . ."

"Yes. In different circumstances. I don't suppose a schoolteacher's salary runs to holiday season trips to winter resorts, does it?" Marcus said, overlooking entirely the presence of her brass-topped friend. "Or to Constanzia Originals?" He didn't look at her as he flipped his cigarette overboard.

"You're utterly hateful, aren't you?" She spoke quietly, as though she were commenting on the weather. "I don't know exactly why you married me, Marcus, or just what you gave up, though I've a good idea. Well, don't worry. As soon as it's reasonably possible, we can get a quiet annulment and go our separate ways. Meanwhile, I'd appreciate it if you'd—"

The sound of several people approaching their sheltered position interrupted her, and she leaned back and closed her eyes as the chatter broke over them both like a warm, friendly wave. She pretended sleep for as long as she could, only opening her eyes when her brass-topped friend touched her shoulder and pointed shoreward.

"Look. El Presidente." She followed his freckled arm to see a large orange-and-purple building looming out of the low-growing vegetation. "For some reason I have yet to fathom, the Mexican people here seem tremendously proud of that hotel. I think I'll have to pay it a visit to see if the inside lives up to the outside. How many orange-and-purple hotels are there in the world, do you suppose, hmmm?"

Kendrik glanced quickly at the next chair. It was

empty. Marcus must have moved, under the cover of the arrival of the others. She hadn't heard him go.

"We're stopping! Is something wrong?" She looked up quickly at her companion.

"As I understand it, this is where we go overboard to explore one of the most famous coral reefs in the area. Are you game? Or is your watchdog still on duty?"

Jumping up quickly, she was suddenly almost overcome with vertigo. Clutching at the arm of the young man beside her, she gasped and laughed up at him. "I didn't eat any breakfast this morning, and a nap in the sun on an empty stomach got to me for just a second." She leaned down to pick up her bag, and as she straightened up she looked directly into the icy blue eyes of her husband. He stared at her for a long moment through the glass windscreen before turning to the vivacious brunette beside him and fitting a mask around her head.

"Come on, Princess! Last one in's a rotten egg!"

Mechanically, she followed her new friend around the narrow walkway to the cockpit.

It was like looking into a blue glass paperweight at a muted but fantastic array of colors. It was impossible to tell if the flickering, jewellike fish were small and close by or huge and far away. Odd-shaped, velvety mounds loomed up on all sides, some covered with tiny, flowerlike growths. Wavy fronds took on an almost animallike appearance. Through this silent dreamscape, masked figures moved in and out of her limited vision. Once she thought she recognized Marcus swimming beneath her, holding the hand of a slender, bikini-clad girl, her dark hair swirling like a smoke cloud behind her. She saw two of the crew members dart into the depths armed with spear guns. Somehow, the thought of violent action in this quiet, blue, fantasy world was unsettling, and she turned and swam back toward the boat.

The strong hands that pulled her over the side remained on her arms as she raised her mask from her face. Salt water ran down into her eyes, bringing tears, and she tried unsuccessfully to wipe them away with the backs of her damp hands. Gratefully, she took the dry handkerchief that was pressed on her and blotted her brow and eyes.

"Thank you," she gasped, looking up at the donor.

Marcus's cool nod as he replaced the handkerchief in the pocket of his terrycloth shirt made her feel somehow awkward and uncertain.

"It was beautiful, wasn't it? I haven't ever been in water quite that clear. Down around Cape Lookout it sometimes calms down so that the visibility is pretty fair, but the scenery can't compare!" She tried to cover up her uneasy feeling by speaking in an unnaturally bright voice. Leaning down to remove her flippers, she was unaware of just when Marcus walked away.

She deliberately chose a seat up close to the cabin, where there was only room for one, and spent the remainder of her time aboard there. She watched with pretended interest as they cruised over a clear, sandy bottom to allow a member of the crew to dive for conchs. She wasn't particularly sorry she couldn't watch him clean them from her vantage spot. Marcus stayed inside talking to the only English-speaking member of the crew until they edged up close to a powdery white beach bordered by a fringe of coconut palms and papaya trees.

Several thatched shacks dotted the area, and she was wondering about the purpose of those and the large, open-sided thatched shelter when she sensed Marcus's presence beside her. She saw his brown, slender feet on the blue-painted deck next to her, and her eyes moved compulsively up the length of his long, powerful legs with their thick covering of brown hair to the brief black trunks topped by the white terry shirt.

"Over you go. We swim from here." He peeled off his shirt and she followed suit. "Shallow dive. It's hard to figure depths in water this clear, so we'd better not take any chances." He was over the side, coming to his feet quickly in shoulder-deep water.

She followed and swam on toward the shore, aware of his brown body lazily knifing the water at her side. They walked up onto the coral sand together, shaking back wet hair simultaneously.

Once ashore, they were told that it would be some time before lunch was ready and that while the crew members set out the supplies provided by the hotel and prepared the fresh seafood, there was plenty of time to swim and to explore the surrounding beaches.

Kendrik and Marcus, with one accord, started walking toward the cool-looking grove of palms that grew out on the nearby point of land.

"There you are! What happened to you? I thought you were going to carry me ashore. You know I can't really swim well without flippers." The girl who had come up behind them so swiftly to clasp Marcus's arm was really lovely, with her sun-bronzed skin, her cloud of dark hair, and her obsidian eyes. She sparkled up at Marcus while ignoring Kendrik's presence completely.

"You seem to have managed pretty well without me."

"Yes, but now that I've found you again I need you to help me do something. Come on, now. I can't reach up high enough, and I need you to boost me."

Kendrik walked on slowly as Marcus paused beside the importunate girl. She looked down at her small feet as they scuffled through the dusty white sand. There were a few shells, nothing really to claim her attention, but she didn't dare look back at the couple engaged in quiet conversation behind her. The brilliant, travel-poster scene made no impression on her at all as she became more and more bogged down in the treacherous quicksand of her own emotions.

It had been only a matter of hours since she had learned the agonizing truth about her marriage. Now the knowledge was etched into her very marrow, and she was beginning to realize that she could no longer stay here, seeing him all day, every day—and night—loving him as she did. She faced the awful sureness that no matter what he did, no matter how little she meant to him, she was irrevocably in love. The knowledge made her feel more alone than she had thought possible.

"Ken, do you want to come with us to see if we can shake down a coconut or two?"

She turned to look back at the striking pair beside the aquamarine water. Her shoulders drooped unconsciously as she mentally compared the dark, vivacious good looks of the girl beside Marcus to her own slender form—colorless, she thought, in her sand-colored bikini that matched her sand-colored hair and her sand-colored skin. The bottle-green eyes tried on a look of cool indifference as she answered, "You go on. I'll walk a while, then probably lie out in the sun." She turned and sauntered casually along the water's edge.

CHAPTER EIGHTEEN

Kendrik had been dozing, lapsing in and out of confused dreams, when she felt an insect crawling on her thigh. Kicking drowsily, she dislodged it and sank back into a warm limbo. Just before her mind could disappear over the far edge of consciousness, the tickling began again in the same place.

"Mmm-hmmf," she muttered and brushed blindly with one hand in the general direction of her thigh.

Her hand encountered a smooth, hot firmness, and she sat up abruptly, blinking at the blinding sun and trying to recognize the looming, dark form beside her. Marcus, she thought.

"This side's well done. Would you care to broil the other side to the same degree of doneness, or will you be content with medium rare?" Her friend of the freckles and brass hair.

"O-o-o-oh! I think well done is an understatement!" She looked with dismay at her midriff, which now contrasted strongly with her beige suit.

"Get back here in the shade, and I'll pour some of my lotion on you. It should take a little of the fire out, at least." He produced a small tube of lotion from his trunks.. "In the middle of the day like this it doesn't take long to blister, even with the vestiges of last year's tan for a base. Of course"—he laughed ruefully—"I wouldn't know about tans from personal experience. My mother ordered a polka-dotted baby with a pun'kin colored top!"

They had reached the shelter of a viridian thicket, and he unscrewed the small plastic tube.

"I'm good for back rubs, but I guess you'd better handle this. On second thought, your shoulders got a little bit, too, even though you were sprawled out on your back, snoring to beat the band!"

"I was not! I would have known if—" She broke off as he started laughing. "Incidentally, Doctor Polka Dot, my name's Kendrik Haynes... Manning. What's yours?"

"Leonard Parkin Dalton, rescuer of fair maids, dispenser of magic potions, instructor of small monsters—at your service." He made an exaggerated bow, then fell in a heap as she pushed him over with one foot.

"All seriousness aside," he said later, clowning, after she had anointed her burning body and returned his tube, "I don't quite know what gives with you and the tall, stern hero type. Is he your husband, your uncle, or keeper, or what?"

"He—he's my husband."

"You don't sound very sure. I gather this is not an affair of long standing.

Though her sunburn covered the blush that flowed up to her face, her downcast eyes gave away her embarrassment.

"I forgot to mention, among my other credentials, one rather bony shoulder for crying upon and one red, slightly bent ear."

The sympathy apparent in his unprepossessing midwestern accent was her undoing. She sobbed once, then broke into childish, noisy tears. He held her and patted her head in awkard silence until she had subsided into hiccups.

"I'm sorry. I don't know what prompted that.... Yes, I guess I do, too," she corrected herself. "But it's something I have to work out for myself." She sat up straight and mopped ineffectively at her tears with a slightly sandy fist.

"It's entirely possible, fair maid, that your recent attack

of vapors was brought on by privation and starvation," Leonard announced, and he stood and pulled her to her feet. "Methinks I detect the redolence of fried fish on the tropic air. C'mon!" He grabbed her by the hand, and they ran, stumbling and laughing, toward the beach, where they turned in the direction of the cook sheds. "Race you."

The meandering crowd around the shelter absorbed their arrival, and Kendrik looked around quickly for Marcus. Not seeing him, she took a seat at one of the long, weathered tables, and Leonard took two paper plates over to the cook shack where lunch was being dispensed. He was back shortly, and as he approached her from the right side, Marcus's voice sounded quietly from her left.

"Here. I've brought your lunch for you. Mexican beer suit you, or would you rather have lemonade?"

"*Cerveza,* by all means." She looked in confusion toward the man on her right, but he winked at her and moved on beyond, hailing a lively group consisting of two men and three girls.

"You disappeared for quite a spell. Looks as if you might have overdone the sunbathing," Marcus said as he split the crisp, brown fish with his hands, deftly removing the bones from each side with one stroke.

"Did you find any coconuts?" Kendrik countered. She poked curiously at an unidentifiable mixture in a paper bowl. "What's this? Do you know?"

"Conch salad. Try it. It's a specialty in this area, and I've never tasted better."

Cautiously, she tasted a small forkful of the dish. "It's delicious! Have you had it before? What's in it?"

Seemingly relieved to find an impersonal topic of conversation, he told her how the large muscle of the conch was chopped fine, marinated in olive oil and lime juice, then mixed with chopped sweet onion, chili pepper, salt, and coarsely ground black pepper.

"It's really raw, then, isn't it?" she asked.

"Not exactly. It's coagulated protoplasm—not cooked by heat, but by the action of the lime juice."

"I'll take your word for it. This is the best beer I've tasted, too. Maybe it's just that everything tastes better out on the beach."

Her mind flew back to another party on another beach. Marcus had brought Scott to her then, but it had already been too late. Any chance of renewed feeling she had had for the younger man had already been dispersed by her growing love for this man beside her.

She applied herself to her lunch and remained silent until Marcus stood and gathered the disposable utensils and the beer bottles.

"I'll take care of these, and I'd advise you to stay out of the sun until time to go back." So saying, he walked away.

Sometime during the night, Kendrik awoke with a pounding headache. As she struggled to sit up in the dark room, she tried to throw off the remnants of a dream, but it kept getting mixed up with the waking nightmare in which she found herself, and she whimpered as she fought the tangle of bedcovers. She was being washed around in a heavy surf, and the sand had scraped all the skin on her body raw. Standing on the shore were Marcus and Erma, and they laughed as they watched her struggling to stand. As she felt herself washing out to sea, unable to fight the fierce currents any longer, she gave one last, despairing cry.

"Marcus!"

A dim, shaded light turned the room into a forest of shadows, and she flinched as a huge, dark form loomed over her.

"Honey, what's wrong? What is it? Are you ill?" The soft, deep voice felt like velvet, and she reached instinctively for its smooth comfort.

"You're burning up!" he cried as he placed a cool hand on her forehead. "Lie down and let's see what we can do to help."

It didn't occur to her in her somnolent state to disobey the gentle, disembodied voice. Her eyes still refused to focus, and her mind was lost somewhere between sleep and wakefulness. She felt cool air strike her body and then something cool, wet, and soft seemed to be extinguishing the fire that raged along her limbs.

"My head hurts," she managed to whisper, and instantly the cool, comforting presence was gone. She felt herself adrift once more, and panic raised her voice as she cried out, "Don't leave me!"

"Sit up, now, honey, and take these. They'll take care of your headache."

Someone lifted her up enough to swallow something, and she eased back down on her pillow, clinging to the hand that supported her.

"Don't go," she murmured, eyes still closed in fevered dreams. As she was swallowed up once more by deep sleep, she felt again the slow, cool, soothing movements up and down her arms and legs and across her burning shoulders.

Much later, she opened her eyes to a silvery grayness. Shivering uncontrollably, she felt around the foot of the bed for a blanket. Surely there was one somewhere! Her hand encountered nothing more than the dry, harsh, cotton seersucker bedspread.

Thoroughly awake now, she looked around the room. In the predawn light she saw the long, irregular ridge in the bed on the other side of the room. Moving as quietly as possible, without taking her eyes from the sleeping form of her husband, she opened her suitcase and pulled out an ivory-colored negligee. Slipping it over her head and putting her arms into the long sleeves, she reached in again, this time drawing out a thick, cotton beach jacket. She pulled this on over the negligee and returned to her bed. Still cold, she got up once more and, finding no blankets, brought several thick towels from the bathroom and spread them over the bed.

Once more huddled under the inadequate pile of covers, she tried vainly to still the chattering of her teeth and to calm the tremors that racked her slender frame. She shut her eyes, squinting them tightly closed, and willed herself to relax.

"You forgot your hat and gloves, honey," Marcus said softly from somewhere behind her back.

Curled as she was into a tight knot, she found that her muscles refused to allow her to turn and look at him. Instead, she cut her eyes around to glimpse his hateful grin gleaming whitely in the shadowed darkness of his face.

"I-it's n-n-not f-funny!" she chattered, frowning at the wall again.

"No, child, I know it's not, but I can't deny you look like an ill-assorted pile from the ragbag." He didn't try to hide his amusement, and she, in her misery, tried to find a scathing reply but lapsed into shuddering silence.

"I doubt that there's a hot-water bottle on the whole of this little sun-baked island, so we'll just have to rough it."

So saying, he eased into the big bed behind her rigid back, and she felt the delicious warmth of him pour over her chilled body. His powerful arm drew the hard knot of her curled-up body back close to him, and as the shudders gradually subsided, she slept.

CHAPTER NINETEEN

The rather ponderous air conditioner was struggling noisily against heavy odds when she awoke. The creaks and rumblings overlaid bursts of childish laughter and the insistent beat of a hard-rock band.

Scattering towels behind her as she walked, Kendrik crossed to the louvered windows and looked outside.

Several boys, the oldest probably not more than ten, were darting from bole to bole of the coconut palms and onto the pile of rocks pushing up from the sand at the edge of the water. They were clad in faded, skimpy bathing trunks and torn-off blue jeans.

Sprawling in well-oiled abandon on the several chaise lounges along the beach were women—girls?—It was hard to distinguish ages, for the minimum attire differed little from body to body. Evidently they were of an age to appreciate rock music, for the cacophony seemed to emanate from that area.

Drawing the curtains over the hastily closed louvers, as though the bright, screen-printed cotton could shut out sound as well as light, she stumbled rather rigidly over to the bamboo settee. Its unyielding surface was distinctly uncomfortable to her tender skin, but she almost welcomed the pain. An anodyne, perhaps? She recalled when, as a child, she suffered some painful cut or bruise, there was inevitably a gleeful offer of help. Want me to help you forget all about that pain? Wait'll I get my hammer! Somewhere in the confused memories of last night, of yesterday and the day before, was the source of a growing ache that rendered insignificant this insistent pain of her burned body.

Did she or did she not remember Marcus holding her

149

close to dispel her chills as she slipped off to sleep last night? Even more nebulous was the vague remembrance of something wet and cool that stroked away the fire from her limbs. But that was—a dream? Was it? She recalled more clearly now his laughing at her, calling her a ragbag, or something, and making her feel quite childish. Funny. She felt anything but childish now.

She stood under a gentle shower for a long time, reveling in its palliative coolness. The pain returned as she slipped on her lightest and silkiest clothing, but along with the tenderness of her skin came a rather spectacular hunger. Remembering that she had had nothing to eat since lunch yesterday, having gone to bed shortly after they had returned to the hotel, she gathered her bag and her sunglasses and went out in search of lunch and of Marcus. Not necessarily in that order. There are hungers and hungers.

Mara called to her from their second-floor balcony as she locked the door behind her, and she looked up to see the three of them, Marcus, Fred, and Mara, looking relaxed and cool under the yellow awning.

"Come on up, Kendrik. We've been watching for you. Have something long, cool, and rummy," Mara offered as Kendrik reached the top of the stairway against the white stucco wall.

"Thanks. But I could do with something long, cool, fruity, and unrummy."

"Here, try this. If you can taste any rum in it, I'll admit it's there. If not, what you don't know won't hurt you." Fred handed her a tall, fruit-garnished glass.

"What time is it?" she asked, still not looking directly at Marcus. "Have I missed lunch yet?"

"No, you're just on time," Fred said. "I'm usually storming the doors by the time they deign to open.

Mealtimes seem to get later and later each day. Mexican *manana,* I suppose."

The light colloquy continued as they finished their drinks, and still Kendrik had neither looked at nor spoken directly to Marcus. This is silly, she told herself. Childish. After all, he is my lawfully wedded husband, no matter how unwilling he is—we are.

They argued amiably over baby shark in tomato sauce versus turtle, and somewhere during the hilarious attempts to translate sections of the menu that were in Spanish, she found herself talking quite easily to Marcus.

"What does this mean in English?" Mara asked their deft, attentive waiter.

"Eet ees a food of the meal of corn with—"

"No, I mean what is the literal translation?" She pointed to the menu, her finger hesitating at each word.

The handsome, dark, Mayan-looking face frowned for a moment, then cleared like a sunburst.

"Ah-h-h." He seemed inordinately pleased at his own astuteness in understanding the peculiarities of the group of North American tourists. "That mean," he said, "the arm of the queen," and once more seemed mystified as they broke into peals of laughter.

As neither Kendrik, with her overdose of sun, nor Mara, with her aversion to the aging rays of ultraviolet, were keen to go snorkling, the four agreed on an easy afternoon spent lazily on the yellow-shaded balcony.

Gradually, they settled into a relaxed, almost lethargic attitude as the desultory hum of conversation thinned under the heavy, humid atmosphere. The yellow canvas awning tinted the late afternoon sun and cast lemon-colored shadows on the white stucco walls.

Fred dozed over his financial reports while Mara and Kendrik swapped comments on resort fashions, a subject new to Kendrik and not particularly absorbing, but one dear to the heart of the other woman.

Under lowered eyelids, Marcus watched the two women, one dramatically beautiful with her stark white complexion, her blue-black hair, and the crimson slash of lipstick that matched her linen dress, the other a complete contrast as she sat in a rather awkward position in the low bamboo chair. Her hair was the color of ripe wheat, its flyaway tendencies encouraged by the salt air. Her tan was overlaid with a reddish glaze that made her eyes seem greener than ever. She had kicked off her sandals, and one toe absently scratched a mosquito bite on the back of the other ankle.

Later on, as the sun paused a moment on the horizon before surrendering to the still waters of the Caribbean, Marcus, standing beside Kendrik's low chair, reached out a finger and lifted a few strands of her gossamer hair. As she became aware of his touch, she drew in her breath quickly and moved back.

Mara, misinterpreting Kendrik's reaction, remarked on her sunburn. "The fewer clothes you wear, the better you'll feel, but I suppose one must bow to convention."

"I seem to stick to every seam that touches me," Kendrik laughed. "I can't think what I'm going to do about dressing for dinner tonight."

"I think I have just the thing," Mara said.

"Oh, no, you mustn't think I meant—"

"Of course not, dear, but it is a problem, and I do have a dress that would be absolutely the most comfortable thing you could possibly wear under the circumstances. Come on, I'll get it for you."

Kendrik looked doubtfully at the other woman. Both were about the same height, but Kendrik's slender, softly rounded figure bore little resemblance to the voluptuous curves of the dark-haired Mara.

"Wait. You'll see." Mara laughed, leading the way into the luxurious bedroom. She crossed the turquoise-carpeted floor and threw open the door to the enormous closet. Color rioted like a flower garden gone wild. Not a gentle little petunia and morning-glory flower bed, but a jungle of canna red, trumpet-vine orange, and passion-flower purple complemented by every imaginable shade of green.

"Poor Fred, he's satisfied as long as his suit and dinner jacket fit well enough not to bind, but he secretly loves to indulge my passion for clothes. Look!" She pulled out a wisp of gossamer chiffon. It looked like a scarf of muted shades of blue and green with an occasional flick of violet, but as she held it up, Kendrik could see that it was actually a triple layer of chiffon, flaring out from the tiny spaghetti straps. There was no waistline to cut into her tender midriff, no seams to chafe, and as Mara remarked, it was opaque enough and flared enough not to need undergarments.

"Oh, Mara, are you sure? It looks fabulously expensive. What if I spill something on it?"

"Don't worry, dear. Actually, it was one of my few errors. I usually stick to my own style and colors, but it looked so ethereal I just couldn't resist. Unfortunately, instead of looking ethereal in it, I looked like a maiden aunt trying to recapture her lost youth." They both laughed at the obvious exaggeration, and once more, Kendrik felt a warm glow of affection for this polished beauty.

"I can't think why you're so good to me. I feel at an utter loss in this place, but you make it all right, somehow."

"Oh, my sweet, why on earth should you feel that way? You have everything any girl should want! If I didn't like you so much, I should probably hate you simply for being ten years younger—all right, fifteen!—than I am, and so lovely along with it! It's easy to see why Marcus finally met his Waterloo!"

"No, no!" Kendrik felt she should somehow make the other woman understand the real situation, but she couldn't think how to begin. Before she could assemble the right words, Mara went on.

"I'd actually begun to wonder if Marcus would ever be caught." Kendrik cringed inwardly at her choice of words. "He's fabulous, of course, quite the handsomest man I think I've ever met, in an utterly masculine way, and all those dull little stocks and bonds didn't do much to make him unpopular, either!"

"What stocks and bonds?" Kendrik asked dumbly.

"Oh, honey! Even you can't be that naive. Why, surely you know Marcus is one of the wealthiest men in the Southeast! I'll admit, he plays it cool with the bird-watching, newspaper-scribbling thing, but all the women who hung around the television crowd trying to get a nod from him knew the signs! The penthouse in Central Park South he was using then, the mountain place in North Carolina I heard about but never saw. Those don't exactly come in Cracker Jack boxes, you know!"

Kendrik sat down suddenly, her legs that had burned a short while ago completely numb now.

"B-but, he lives in my grandfather's old place. It only has f-five rooms, and—and he drives a Travelall that has some rust on it." She grasped at straws, trying to find her balance in an unsteady world that had tilted yet again. She looked up with a pleading expression on her face, as if hoping for a denial of the things she had just heard.

"Then it's even worse than I thought," Kendrik whispered almost to herself.

"What's worse, dear?" asked Mara, trying to close the

closet door without catching a jade-green skirt in the crack.

Before Kendrik could speak, Marcus appeared in the door.

"Have you gone to sleep? Come on, Kendrik. We'll go for a short stroll along the beach now that the sun's gone down. I need some exercise before dinner."

Kendrik stood up and moved toward the door like a sleepwalker, still unable to assimilate all she had just heard.

"Don't forget your dress. It's yours to keep, remember, and I wouldn't be surprised at seeing you live in it for the next few days. It's really tacky on me, but quite the most comfortable thing I've ever worn."

CHAPTER TWENTY

By unspoken consent, both Marcus and Kendrik slipped off their shoes, and Marcus dropped those and the dress inside their door as they passed.

"I'm glad we have this room right on the beach," Marcus said as they walked the few yards to the water's edge.

Kendrik didn't comment, still wrapped up in trying to take in the new picture of her husband. That he was successful as a writer, she knew, but writers don't make fortunes. At least, not wildlife writers for moderate-sized newspapers. The air of success, of authority, the assurance she had been aware of from the very first were explained now, but the knowledge cast him into a new light. More than ever, he was Marcus the cosmopolite, the playboy surrounded by beautiful, talented, wealthy women—the Ermas, the Maras.

An unbidden sigh left her, and she hunched her shoulders and clasped her upper arms, chilled slightly by her own unflattering self-appraisal as well as by the little breeze that had sprung up.

"Cold?" Marcus asked her, slowing his steps as they neared the mound of rocks that loomed ahead of them at the edge of the water.

"No. Not really. Can we sit here for a while?" She leaned against the closest of the boulders, appreciating the stored heat of the sun, and he lifted her up to sit on its rounded dome. He took a seat on the next one and drew up his knees, clasping his strong arms around them.

"We seem to be slipping farther and farther apart in our relationship," he began abruptly. "Somewhere along the line something happened, something that made you—

distrust me. I need to know, Kendrik, if we're ever going to get on an even keel again." He looked at her, seeing the aureole caused by the sun's afterglow shining through her hair. "I'm still the same man who married you, and you're still the same girl I married, so what's wrong?"

She turned to him, her eyes large in the fading light. "Marcus." She paused and bit her lip, not knowing where to start. "I've got to know why—"

"Hey, you two! Where have you been all day? You're missing all the fun!" Several people converged around the little pile of rocks, among them Leonard Dalton and the smoky-haired brunette. "C'mon, we've got something going on the next point. You're just in time!"

The tanned, dark-haired girl put a hand on the back of Marcus's neck, tickling his hair lightly.

"You're going to spoil my evening if you say no, Marc. You wouldn't want to do that, would you?" She bent her face over and whispered something in his ear, laughing as her hand slid from his neck on down to his arm.

"Kendrik?" Marcus looked over at her with a rather enigmatic expression. "Shall we go for a few minutes?"

"Oh, don't worry about your little friend," the brunette said. "Leonard here has been positively pining for her all day. She's monopolized you long enough, anyway." She looked at Kendrik, and her playful smile turned into something not quite so friendly. "You two don't play fair. You must mix it up, you know. We can't let you walk off with all the goodies."

"I think you're right, Mitzi. Kendrik has a way with schoolteachers, did you know? Yes, she attracts them like bees to nectar, don't you, Kendrik?" He lifted her down and deliberately turned to the other girl, leaving Kendrik completely nonplussed.

Her feelings of bewilderment lasted only a split second,

however, before temper pushed them aside. Casting the slightly apologetic-looking Leonard a very provocative look from under her lashes, she tucked a hand under his arm.

"Rescued in the nick of time, brave knight!" Fortunately, it was too dark by now for him to see the gleam of tears in her eyes.

"Don't mind Mitzi too much, gal. She's a good sport." Where had Kendrik heard that term before? Good sport, indeed. How could men be so stupidly blind where women were concerned? Pythons were good sports, too, no doubt.

"Oh, I don't mind! I suppose it's silly, going off alone together—with your own husband. I-I mean, just how ridiculous can you get?" She gulped back tears of disappointment.

"Mitzi doesn't mean any permanent harm. I think she must have recognized your husband from somewhere, the way she locked her radar in on him and took aim. He's not a movie star, I suppose? I only recognize the female ones, of course. Bachelor's rule number seventeen."

Kendrik had recovered her equilibrium by the time they reached the campfire around the rocky point of beach. Leonard led her to a large beach towel and held her hand as she lowered herself gingerly to the ground. She looked around for Marcus, but he, evidently, had taken a detour. So that was the way wealthy playboy husbands acted on their honeymoons. Okay. She had thought she was getting a lonely man who needed a wife and a home to take away the memory of a miserable boyhood, but as he'd said, it was a whole new ballgame.

Only she didn't know the rules, she only knew that she couldn't play by those that seemed to be in effect. Hastily she quelled the small internal voice that said, Honeymoon? Are you sure you're playing the game at all? Maybe this isn't what Marcus had in mind when he married you, either.

Looking at the laughing faces around the campfire, she was back for an instant in her nightmare of the night before. Erma and Marcus were laughing at her as she struggled to stand in the overwhelming currents. She shivered.

"Who plays this thing? My fingers are all thumbs," someone said.

"No they're not, it's your brain! It's all beer!" another voice laughed.

"Here, pretty li'l gal, I'll just bet you play," the first voice said. Someone thrust a guitar at her, and rather than let it drop into the sand, she took it. Looking at the lightly bearded young man, she asked, "What would you like to sing?"

Several voices chimed in at once, requesting various tunes. She selected one and began to strum softly. One of the girls had a truly lovely voice, and it lifted above the others and knit together the mixture of tone-deaf and tipsy choristers. She played several more popular tunes, all known to at least two or three of the group.

As the consumption of beer increased, the quality of the singing decreased, and Kendrik began one of her own favorites, an old ballad of unknown origin. She picked the melody softly for a few bars, humming for a while before she found herself singing the half-forgotten words of the last verse.

I'll set sail with silver and steer t'wards the sun,
I'll set sail with silver and steer t'wards the sun,
But my false love will weep, my false love will weep,
My false love will weep for me after I've gone.

Looking around for the case, she quietly replaced the

guitar. Leonard seemed to have succumbed to the beer and the music and, perhaps, the soporific air and was snoring softly. As she started back, she could see two people silhouetted against the lights from the hotel, but there was no way of knowing whether one of them was Marcus.

She hoped not. She didn't want to see him just now, for as she'd sung the words of the lovely old ballad, she had known what she had to do.

Unlocking the door to the suite, Kendrik breathed a sigh of relief that Marcus was not there. Not that he would be, of course. He was somewhere on the beach with that ... that ... Mitzi!

She went swiftly to his open suitcase and felt in the little pouch in the top. There, in a leather folder, were the tickets and tourist cards. She slipped out her own and replaced the folder as she had found it.

Most of her things were still in her suitcase. Only her dresses hung in the closet. She had always had an aversion to putting her personal items of clothing in the dresser drawers of an impersonal hotel room.

On the point of gathering her dresses from the closet, she thought of schedules and reservations. Funny, at a moment like this, her practicality seemed to desert her.

Picking up the phone, she asked to be put through to the airport. It seemed to take forever before she finally reached someone who spoke a smattering of English that jibed with her scanty Spanish. Her fingers danced a little dance of nerves as she ascertained that there was a flight out at five in the morning and that, yes, she could have a seat.

She was in the bathroom when she heard Marcus's key in the door. Her mind flew over details of the room. Had she left any sign of her plans? Any indications of hasty packing? No. There had been no time to start packing. Not that it would take but a minute, anyway. If necessary, she could leave behind some of her things. She probably would have no use for most of them. Not the long white wool, or the chiffon Mara had given her. No, the outer banks of North Carolina would welcome her in her old jeans and her faded tops. Charlie would love her no matter how plain she looked. She was beginning to feel quite sorry for herself when she was roused from her welter of self-pity by a sharp rap on the door.

"Kendrik? Are you in there? If we're going to get any dinner tonight, I'll have to get in."

"Dinner?" She sounded as if he were suggesting some obscure rite she had never heard of. "Oh, dinner! I thought we'd missed it, and I didn't know if you wanted to go to town." Her voice sounded amazingly natural to her own ears.

"It's only a few minutes past nine. Seems later, I know. When did you manage to escape from your schoolteacher friend?"

"Earlier than you escaped from your—your octupus friend!"

There was a low chuckle from the other side of the door. "Come on, now—unless Montezuma has you in his clutches?"

She gasped, then opened the door with rather more force than was really necessary and marched past him, her head in the air.

"Aren't you going to dress for dinner? I was looking forward to seeing you in that little blue flimsy you got from Mara. I suspect it would feel lots better than what you're wearing."

For the first time in several hours, Kendrik became aware of her extreme discomfort. Prickles of perspiration and an inordinate amount of sand seemed suddenly to have sprung up under her wrinkled dress, and she was instantly quite miserable.

"Well, if you don't take all night, maybe there'll be time for me to take a shower," she snapped.

Marcus laughed as he closed the door. "Shave and a shower, five minutes," he announced.

Kendrik moved quickly to transfer her extra sandals from the closet to the suitcase. Every little bit she could do now would make it that much easier to get away quietly in the morning. She considered what to wear tomorrow on the long flight home.

"It's all yours. Ten minutes maximum, okay?" Marcus said.

Silently, she grabbed up her things and strode past him. For some unaccountable reason, the slightly smug expression on Marcus's face made her more angry than ever. If she had not definitely made up her mind to leave before, she would have now. Yes, he would look smug. Beautiful, glamorous women falling out of the woodwork wherever he went. But on his own honeymoon—that was too much! Let Erma fight off the Mitzis and the... yes, probably the Maras, too. She certainly wouldn't join the queue. She pushed back the niggling little doubt that arose in her mind. What if she was being unfair—well, a little bit unfair? But you're *not* being unfair, she told herself. Enough was enough!

Dinner that night was more enjoyable than she had expected. By being rather later than usual, they seemed to be dining with a whole different set of people. As they shared a table for four with an attractive couple who were just a bit past middle age, Kendrik actually found herself entering into a spirited discussion of the merits of state-supported day-care centers by the time they had reached the dessert course.

The older couple, Ed and Martha Blair, were in the administrative end of education, and Kendrik's own knowledge of the subject was based on her father's experience as well as her own independent mind.

"But with the taxpayers crying, 'enough, enough,' and the school system lopping off program after program for lack of funds, how on earth can you condone adding still another load to the already overburdened schools?" Kendrik asked.

"My dear girl, you have a very valid point, but you must remember two things: we in school administration are building our own empires, just as do men in all other endeavors. I expect the real reason I'm interested in day-care centers, though, are their popularity with the younger voters, those who want or need an additional breadwinner in the family and can't afford to pay for someone to keep the children while mother works." Ed Blair smiled his warm smile at the lovely young woman sitting across from him. Her sunburn had faded into a rich, pinkish tan, and the airy drift of blue-green she was wearing seemed almost too frivolous for the earnest expression on her face.

"Young lady, you're entirely too pretty to carry such a burden in your mind. Time enough for you to start thinking of such things when you're a mother yourself and have several little Mannings hanging on to your skirts—or blue jeans, I guess it is, today."

The friendly exchange of information earlier in the evening had elicited the fact that there were no Manning children yet. Kendrik was sure, however, that the Blairs didn't suspect their newlywed status. For one thing,

Marcus, though perfectly polite and charming to the older couple, was being rather distant toward Kendrik. He seemed content to sit back and watch her through narrow-slitted eyes, his expression baffling, to say the least.

He stirred himself and reached for his cup of rich, Mexican coffee as he spoke. "Sometimes a schoolroom, no matter how inept the teacher is, is preferable to the home environment, wouldn't you say, Kendrik?"

She was surprised to hear him speak of his own experience, for he was by nature a reticent man, but he continued. "Kendrik had some small experience recently when a very dear friend of hers, a combination teacher-social worker"—Martha interrupted softly with the comment that they all were—"took into his home several children from troubled homes." He continued, "I believe my wife proved invaluable to him in dealing with the situation."

Kendrik made a deliberate effort to hide her surprise. Had Marcus actually been jealous of her relationship with Jeff? From his odd tone of voice, he seemed to be inferring a great deal more than he said.

Suddenly, Martha Blair broke into her thoughts, saying, "As delightful as the evening has been, you must excuse us." She looked warmly at her husband, with more than a little mischief in her eyes. "We have a little ritual, you see. When we were first married, Ed agreed to indulge me in my passion for walking if I would pander to his delight in lying back with his eyes closed while someone read poetry to him. We were quite different types, you know. I was the outdoor person, while Ed didn't care if he never stuck his nose outdoors. At any rate, we've stuck to our bargain all these years. After dinner, we go for a stroll in all but the most inclement weather, and then we settle down comfortably while I read to him from his favorite books. Of course, I have the better end of the deal—after our walks, he falls asleep before I get to the end of the first page." She laughed openly as Ed Blair swatted at her.

"How about our following their lead and going for a walk?" Marcus asked as they stood outside the dining room looking over the calm sea on which mingled the reflections of starlight and the incandescent lights from the shore.

Thinking about what Martha had said about Ed's propensity for falling asleep after they returned from their walks, Kendrik murmured agreement and went willingly as Marcus tucked her hand under his white-clad arm.

They walked silently until they had passed their own hotel and that next door to them. They were on a so-called unimproved section of the beach, near the site of the earlier party, before the silence was broken.

"This is dangerous, you know," remarked Marcus.

"How so?" Kendrik returned from her world of nebulous daydreams concerning this man at her side.

"Well, can you think of a more potent combination than a balmy night beside a tropical sea and a lovely young woman by your side?" He stopped and turned her to face him.

"Even if the so-called lovely young woman is the wife of the handsome, mysterious man?" she said.

"Especially if the lovely young woman is the wife of the so-called handsome, mysterious man."

His eyes asked a question of her as he held her loosely before him. She wanted nothing more than to answer that question with all the love in her heart, but she, too, was aware of the dangers. In the stillness of the black, transparent night, she heard her own heart pounding out an insistent rhythm. The gentle fingers of the wind lifted and swirled the gossamer chiffon about her body, and she felt herself being drawn into a world ruled by the senses instead of the mind.

Closer he came, his arms compelling her as his mouth hovered a breath away from her own.

"Hey, man, y' gotta match? Fire went out an' everybody went off an' lef' me here!"

Kendrik sprang away, shock pouring like ice through her veins. Marcus's voice was barely recognizable as he swore fluently under his breath. He grabbed her by the arm and virtually dragged her along as his long legs ate up the distance between them and their hotel room.

"Marcus, wait! You're hurting me!" she panted. Instantly he slowed his stride, allowing her to catch up with him and regain her balance. Already the inebriated survivor of the party was left far behind.

Wow! That was a near thing, old girl, she told herself. Dangerous is right! Aloud she said, "Why don't we go see if Fred and Mara are still up? I'd like to—to say—to see them," she faltered. It would never do to go directly to the room now, not if she ever meant to leave.

They had reached the paved walkway through the sand and they could turn left and enter their own room, turn right and stop in the bar where the indefatigable Mexican trio was holding forth, or go up the stairs before them to the balcony that opened into the Kleins' suite.

Marcus paused, still holding her arm, and looked down at her averted face. A shadow from a dry, rustling palm frond threw his own face in shadow, and even if she had dared to look, it's unlikely she could have read his expression.

For what seemed like a century to Kendrik, but was no more than a few seconds, he continued to study the girl before him. She seemed strangely insubstantial in her

wisps of moonlit chiffon, related only by a waft of her
favorite perfume to the flesh-and-blood woman of the
homey little cottage by the Atlantic.

"Yes. All right, if that's really what you want to do." He
glanced up at the light pouring from the sliding glass door
onto the open balcony. Taking her arm once more, he led
her up to the door of suite 205.

CHAPTER TWENTY-ONE

"My name is really Mary. I don't mind admitting it, I just don't want to be called by it." The three other people lounging around the attractive room with tall glasses in their hands laughed at Mara's revelation. Kendrik protested that Mary was one of the loveliest names of all.

"Too ordinary by far for my Mara. Yes, under all the heavy, expensive gift paper and fancy ribbons you find a comfortable, frumpy housewife, wrinkled stockings, rundown felt slippers, and all." Fred leaned away as Mara made a threatening gesture.

"How about Marcus?" Mara countered. "I've seen him dressed to the teeth in white tie leading a covey of high muckety-mucks into Kennedy Center and dashing around New York State in that navy blue Morgan of his with—what's her name, Marcus? That singer—Bobbie Lee something or other. Anyway," she continued without pausing for an answer, "Fred, remember when we dropped in on him unexpectedly in Norfolk and found him sitting on the bathroom floor with the plumbing all scattered around him in a hundred pieces?"

Marcus threw back his head and laughed, the open white collar and loosened tie revealing his sinewy brown throat. "I was trying to retrieve an assortment of articles the Jacobsens' boy—he must have been about three then—tried to flush. Scientific experiment, no doubt."

Kendrik followed the conversation without contributing more than an occasional comment. Looking from one of them to the other, three attractive individuals discussing fascinating people she had never met and well-known places she had never seen, she felt more than ever out of her element.

Imperceptibly, the hum of conversation became only a background for her own thoughts, and she found herself remembering an incident that had happened the summer she was eleven. Since her real birthday tended to get lost in the excitement of Christmas, she always had a half-birthday party in June, on the island. Her half-birthday party had included, as did most of the children's parties on the island, all the children of the appropriate age. There was a girl—Kendrik couldn't even remember her name, but she had come, walking from the farthest end of the village in her cheap, ugly dress and her outgrown, worn-out shoes with her gift in a string-tied brown paper bag. She stood in the door, looking pale and frightened and ready to run when she caught sight of the other children in their party clothes with their beribboned gifts. One boy—she had an awful feeling it might have been Buck Hollis—caught sight of the paper bag and ran toward her, a stick leveled over his shoulder, and with a loud war whoop, he speared the bag, spilling walnuts all over the floor. About a pound or two of walnuts. The other children screamed with laughter, and Kendrik looked into the face of the daunted girl for a long moment before turning to the others with a cry.

"Help me, everyone! I haven't had a walnut in ages, and they're absolutely my favorite food! If you let one single walnut escape, I'll never forgive you!" She was on her knees poking under the heavy old mission furniture. "I didn't know there was a single walnut on the island this time of year!"

All during the party Kendrik ate walnuts, loudly and not very subtly appreciative, until the poor girl was quite convinced that her gift had been a stroke of genius. After the party Kendrik was very sick in her stomach.

Now, why did I think of that incident? I'm sure I

haven't thought of it since it happened. And then it came to her. She knew exactly how that girl had felt. Facing the laughter of those well-dressed children as she stood there, her poverty exposed to all, her paltry gift torn away, she had known, as Kendrik knew now, the terrible pain of having nothing of value to give.

Mara stifled a yawn, and instantly Marcus was on his feet. "Come on, Ken. If that's not a broad hint, I don't know one when it's presented."

Mara laughed protestingly, but Fred put an arm about her shoulder and said to the two guests, "She played poker until almost two this morning. Poker, mind you! I dropped out about midnight, and this morning she wouldn't even tell me whether she won or lost."

"You play poker using corporations for chips. Don't you dare fuss at me for playing for matches!" Mara said.

"We'll see you in the morning, all right? There's a pretty fair tennis court around here somewhere, or we could go to the other side of the island hunting Mayan ruins, if you're feeling adventurous. There are several, I understand, but you have to find them for yourself." Fred kissed Kendrik lightly on the cheek, then turned to Marcus and shook his hand. They left in a chorus of good nights.

"You like them, don't you, Ken?" Marcus asked her as he unlocked their door. "I've known them for several years now, and they're really tops on my list of favorite people."

"Yes, I do. They're not like anyone I've ever known before, but I like them tremendously—Mara, especially."

Marcus placed a rather tentative hand on her shoulder. "Would you like a nightcap before we turn in, Ken? I can have something sent over from the bar."

She avoided his eyes and moved away from his touch.

"I—I think I'll just take some aspirin and go to bed, Marcus. It's been such a long day, and my head's beginning to throb."

Marcus surveyed her coolly, his hands on his hips. "Oh, yes. The headache," he said. "Well, you just jump right in, sweetheart. I think I'll go out for a spell. Shame to waste a trip like this!"

She snatched her gown from the door and quickly turned into the bathroom. As she did, she heard the outer door slam behind her and the sound of angry footsteps on the sandy concrete outside.

Before going to bed, Kendrik put all her dresses into her suitcase. She gathered her toilet articles and got together everything she needed to take tomorrow, ready to grab quickly and quietly in the dark. She set her mental alarm clock for three-thirty.

She lay there in the darkness for a long time before she realized that every muscle in her body was tensed. As she made a deliberate effort to relax, the rigid control she had been under gave way, and tears streamed down her face. She buried her head under her pillow to quiet her sobs while she forced herself to face the decision she had made.

I have no choice, she thought. I'll never love another man as I do Marcus, but I have nothing of value to offer him. He's only pretending to like walnuts to save my feelings, but he'll be sick later, sick at heart as I am now. The only thing I can give him is his freedom to marry Erma—to pick up the plans they were forced to drop when he had to marry me. A fresh paroxysm of weeping shook her frail shoulders, but self-pity couldn't last long in an essentially healthy climate and she soon sat up and blew her nose. As she sat there, knees drawn up before her, staring into the dim bedroom, she knew what she had to do.

Jumping out of bed, she pulled her nightgown off and stuffed it into her suitcase, fastening the latch securely. She dressed quickly in a cotton shift and sandals and gathered her things from the bathroom. With one ear out for the sound of gritty footfalls outside, she stuffed the bedclothes with a row of pillows and towels until it approximated her own sleeping form. Then, grabbing her bags, she opened the door and left.

Not until she was safely aboard the Miami-bound jet did she let her rigid backbone droop with weariness and relief. It had not been that difficult to order a taxi to take her to the airport, where she dozed until her plane was loading. But at every turn she had half expected Marcus to appear. Sitting in a window seat on the half-empty plane, she admitted to herself that she had hoped he would stop her.

How could she realistically suppose that she could get up in the middle of the night, dress, gather her things, and leave with Marcus sleeping in the same room? No, you can rationalize all you want to up to a point, she told herself, but beyond that it's lying. You wanted Marcus to discover you in flight and plead with you to come back, now didn't you?

Sleep crowded out self-examination about halfway across the Gulf of Mexico, and she was still groggy when they landed at Miami International. Red-eyed and rumpled, she joined the stream of tourists, most of them heavily laden with straw hampers, colorful paper bags, and other indications of holiday purchases. I wasn't even there long enough to get my money changed, she thought. At least customs will be a snap.

Cashing her last traveler's check, she bought several magazines and was first in line to board the flight to

Atlanta and from there to Norfolk. As they headed north over the flat, green country with the checkerboard design of parking lots and bungalows, her magazines slid from her lap and her eyes closed once more in sleep.

It was heavily overcast by the time they landed in Norfolk, and Kendrik was shocked to be plunged into the midst of winter. Realizing she had left her coat in Marcus's car when they headed south, she hurried to the ladies' lounge and shuffled through her bag for the warmest thing she could find; a long-sleeved knit shirt and the cotton beach jacket.

"Well, the layered look is supposed to be good, but I somehow doubt this is what they have in mind." She spoke aloud as she looked at herself in the mirror of the empty room.

"Bus station?" a taxi driver said a few minutes later. "Okay, Miss. Bags in with you, and I'll save my bursitis a soaking." A steady drizzle had just started.

"Will we be there by—" She tried to see her watch in the flickering lights of traffic but gave up and lapsed into silence. It didn't make much difference. She had no idea what time the bus to Manteo ran, anyway. Closing her eyes, she leaned back in the tobacco-smelling taxi. It's too quick, she thought. I know now what they mean by jet lag.

"Been south, little lady? Some tan y'got there. I been to Florida once—Disney World. Yep. That's some kind of place! One of these days I'm going to the real one. The one in California." His voice droned on against a background of slapping windshield wipers and flickering lights.

"Here ye go, little lady. Airport to bus station in one swell foop." He laughed immoderately at his spoonerism and tipped his hat as he pocketed his money.

The bus ride from Norfolk to Manteo on a rainy night in February is about as far removed from Cozumel as it's possible to get, thought Kendrik as she sat, wide awake, in the high seat of the bus. Here I slept through the Gulf of Mexico, through Florida, Georgia, and South Carolina and I'm wide awake and ready for sightseeing in Moyock, Coinjock, Spot, and Mamie. And in the middle of the night!

Like silent ghosts, the solitary farm houses flashed by in darkness. She saw nothing of the wide expanse of water they crossed over as they neared Kitty Hawk. Kendrik felt a little like a traveler in outer space as she sped along through the silent darkness of winter, still wearing the clothes she had put on in Mexico less than twenty-four hours ago.

She walked from the tiny bus station in Manteo to the service station where she had left her car. It struck her suddenly that the last time she had driven the Bluebird she had been Kendrik Haynes. Now she was Mrs. Marcus Manning. Kendrik Manning, walking alone in the rainy winter night in her mismatched summer clothes, swinging a suitcase! Well, not exactly swinging—dragging would be more like it. The damn thing was heavy!

She unlocked the car and shoved the bag into the back seat. After checking the gas gauge, she tried the starter. Weather like this was not conducive to quick starts, but after several minutes of grinding, the reluctant starter finally caught. She pulled out into the empty street and headed for the outer banks.

CHAPTER TWENTY-TWO

I've crossed a lot of bridges, she thought as she crossed the dawn-tipped water below her. Currituck Sound and marriage and the Gulf and leaving Marcus and Oregon Inlet and—what?

As she drove along the black asphalt ribbon that centered the narrow strip of sand, often catching sight of the sound on one side of her and the ocean on the other, she began to wonder for the first time since fleeing Cozumel just what was in store for her. Her nest egg had been all but expended on her trousseau. It hurt to think of the dreams she had had when she packed the lacy gown Mrs. O'Neal had picked out for her, and the white nylon. She shivered in the dark, steamy interior of the little gray car. The heater made scant progress against the cold of the drizzle that was delaying daylight.

No maudlin self-pity. You're a big girl now. Think of the practical side of things, like no food in the cottage, plumbing all drained, electricity to turn on, Marcus with his arms around your shoulders whispering against your lips—no! Like—like explaining to the O'Neals and the Hollises why she was home alone, where Marcus was.

As she crossed over in the battered old ferry, she looked out over the stern and pictured the gulls that followed the wake in the summertime, often almost landing on the hands that held up scraps to feed them. She wondered idly if Marcus had any theories about a new generation of seagulls that never learned how to find food except at the hands of the tourists. He had told her once about the scientists who had performed autopsies on flocks of birds, only to find they had died with their crops filled with peanut butter. Horrors! Snap out of it, Kendrik. Just because you're tired, bone weary, in fact, cold, hungry—yes, damn it. That's it! When was the last time she had eaten? About Atlanta, wasn't it?

She scrambled through the glove compartment, pulling out roadmaps, registration slip, windshield scraper, one black glove, several packets of salt and one of catsup, an envelope with a phone number on it. Whose? she wondered. No telling. Well, no food.

Daylight was forcing its way weakly through the layer of heavy, low rainclouds when she headed down the last stretch of blacktop. It was not as cold here on the banks as it was on the mainland, thanks to the proximity of the Gulf Stream, several miles offshore, and the surrounding water, which didn't change temperature as rapidly as the air. Cold enough, though, with this northeast wind whipping across the low-lying reef of land. Winter gales had stripped the seed heads from the sea oats and left the bare stalks to act as weather vanes. Dotted here and there were the dark forms of wind-sculpted yaupon and cedar and an occasional scrub oak clinging tenuously to the sand.

The boxy little shingled cottage had never looked so good to the weary girl as when she pulled up close to it on that empty, bleak morning. She sat for a minute in the car mentally reviewing the checklist. Food to buy, mail to check, power to be turned on. First, though, to get out of these wrinkled, dirty, summer clothes and into some warm work clothes.

Running up the slatted wooden porch, she thought of Charlie as she fumbled around for her keys. It would be so good to see him again, although unless she found some sort of job soon, she couldn't afford to feed him. Kendrik herself could manage quite well on eggs, fish, and vegetables, all of which were easy to come by and not very dear, but Charlie, with his voracious appetite, was another matter!

Hauling her suitcase into the dark, thoroughly chilled bedroom, she plopped it on the bed. Freezing fingers made hard work of unlocking it, but finally it opened to reveal the scrambled, hastily packed contents. She fancied she could detect the aroma of oleanders and sunshine clinging to the dress she had packed last of all, the few ounces of blue-and-green chiffon Mara had given her. Sighing, she held it up and looked at it.

Memories came rushing in before she could slam the door. She visualized Mara and Fred and Marcus—and Mitzi? They'd probably go ruin hunting today. Or was that yesterday? Marcus would have thought of some excuse for her absence. Called home by a sick aunt. A sick dog? "A sick heart," she whispered to the empty little room.

Laying aside the dress, she dug into her dresser drawer for a pair of blue jeans and a warm, heavy knit top. Somehow, climbing into the scruffy old black turtleneck top, tight and tattered though it was, did something for her morale, and she felt more like the old Kendrik as she located her tools in the odd little tool closet hidden behind the bathroom door. Picking up the two fuses from where she had left them on the living-room table, she went outside and plugged them into the fusebox on the protected side of the house.

She raced back in and turned on the furnace, listening to its grumbling protestations for a minute before going out again to crawl up under the house. Her mental list led her from valve to valve, and with the help of a heavy wrench, she turned the valves as she went. Scrambling out, she paused for a moment, silently checking off that job and going on to the next. Water. The water meter was out by the road, and she had cut it off before she left so that if anything froze and sprang a leak, she wouldn't be faced with a tremendous water bill. It took only a few minutes to lift the wooden cover and turn the proper things in the proper direction. Now. What next?

She stood there in the damp, blowy cold, idly rubbing her stomach for a minute until she realized what the next item on the list was. Food! It must have been almost a million hours since she had had anything except gallons of coffee and one desiccated pimento cheese sandwich.

Walking back across the ridge upon which the cottage was built, she paused, arms wrapped around her body for warmth, and savored the familiar air. Salt, predominately, with that tinge of iodine that always seemed to accompany sea air. Sea life in all stages of preservation—or lack of it. Closer by, the wet pine straw underfoot, the mushroomy smell of rich humus, and the odd nuances that always seemed to her to come from some exotic country across the Atlantic.

Hurrying up the steps, cold and hunger driving away further appreciation of the island ambience, she opened the door to a downpour.

An upspout was probably a more accurate description, she decided after her initial wet wail.

"Oh, hell! Why, why, why?" She grabbed the nearest thing she could reach to stem the tide. It happened to be a raincoat that was hanging on the peg beside the door, and she thought, wryly, that it would have done much more good on her back.

Thoroughly drenched now, she grabbed the wrench and screwdriver and dashed out again. As she knelt over the meter box, clumsy in her haste to turn off the water again, it started to rain in earnest. It was the grim, resigned, forever kind of gray rain that seemed almost a comment on her life at this point.

Back in the house, she surveyed the damage caused by one valve she'd neglected to turn before she left. One pipe still had water in it when she'd gone—and the water had frozen during her absence, causing a rupture.

The ruptured copper pipe dripped disconsolately as she mopped up the flooded floor. Crawling on her hands and knees, she reached under the odd assortment of furniture that had found its way into the room, coming back again and again to the area beneath the dribbling pipe. Impatiently, she sat up, cracking her head on the bottom of the porcelain basin.

As she instinctively threw up her hand to the offended area, her arm brushed by the ruptured pipe, its sharp edges catching her just below the elbow. The sweater was no protection at all from the jagged metal, and she felt the tear in her arm as her hand held the rising knot on her head.

Leaning up against the wet wall, she let it all out. The pain, the cold, the hunger, and as if that weren't enough to feed her anguish, she thought of all the years ahead of coping alone with just such things.

Putting her head down on her arms, which rested on her drawn-up knees, she gave vent to the misery that had followed her to the Caribbean island and then accompanied her back to this dreary, lonely, awful place. This—this enemy, this—this hateful cottage! She wailed and wept with complete abandon, noisily muttering curses and dire threats against no one in particular, interspersed with loud, shuddering sobs.

She failed to hear the sound of an approaching vehicle. She didn't hear the door of a car slam shut, or the footsteps that pounded up the wet, wooden steps. She only looked up when she became aware of a pair of size-eleven handsewn moccasins almost touching her own wet, sandy sneakers. Her eyes traveled up an improbable length of gray flannel that only hinted at the powerful muscles beneath, to a heavy, knit pullover, and beyond that to—

"Marcus!" She looked up at his grim face and saw the deep concern written in his eyes and broke into wails all over again. "Oh, Marcus, I'm so hungry," she sobbed incoherently. "I love you so much and I'm so tired and so cold and, Marcus, the pipe burst and—"

"Sweetheart, precious, don't." Warm hands lifted her up and strong arms gathered her close as his warm breath stirred the damp tendrils of hair on her nape.

He held her gently and whispered things she only dimly understood until her sobs diminished. Then, placing a dry handkerchief in her grubby hand, he led her into the living room. He pushed her gently into a chair, produced another clean handkerchief, and tied it around her arm where the pipe had cut her. Then he disappeared in the direction of the bedroom, only to reappear a moment later carrying her suitcase and her handbag.

"Where are we going?" Her eyes were round above tear-stained, slightly dirty cheeks.

"We're going home, darling." He took her hand and pulled her toward the door, reaching behind him to turn out the light. "Don't talk. Don't even think. Just relax and try not to worry about a thing now."

Her eyes never left his face, her expression one of utter bafflement as she watched him start his car and drive a cool ten miles above the speed limit with great skill and equally great unconcern.

They pulled up in front of the familiar bungalow before she could formulate a single question, and then it was too late. Marcus led her inside, dumped her suitcase on the bed, and opened the bathroom door, where he started a gushing flow of hot, steamy water in the tub.

"Strip!" he ordered and reached for her as she stood motionless. "You have exactly fifteen minutes before omelets, coffee, and toasted muffins are ready."

That did it. As he closed the door behind him with a firm hand, she peeled off her soggy, ripped sweater and stepped out of wet sneakers, jeans, and yesterday's briefs all in one motion. She inspected the cut on her arm and found it was just superficial, painful more than anything else. Pouring most of a bottle of bath crystals into the tub, she grabbed a bottle of shampoo before submerging her whole wet, tired, cold, dirty body in the marvelous, steamy, fragrant tub.

Looking around for something to put on before venturing out of the bathroom, her eyes lighted on a familiar blue terrycloth wrap hanging on the back of the door. She grinned as she knotted the sash around her middle, turning up the cuffs to reveal her water-wrinkled fingertips.

She had barely time to towel her hair briskly, setting wispy little curls on end all around her face as she twisted the long ends into a knot on top of her head. The steamy mirror revealed only a faceless, rosy-tan creature with a delicate little neck rising from a huge, enveloping swath of blue. The unreasonable lift to her spirits had nothing at all to do with her looks, or her empty stomach, either.

Following the sumptuous aroma of freshly made coffee, she opened the kitchen door, only to be assailed by shyness at the sight of the rangy, rugged man setting the table with delicate, violet-sprigged china. In the center of the scrubbed, wooden table was a dark green bottle of waxy, gray bayberries. Beside it was another bottle, which Marcus lifted and poured as she approached.

"To us?" His eyes held a question as he passed her the glass of sparkling white wine.

"Yes. To us," she whispered shyly, raising her glass to his.

"Marcus," she ventured some time later as they sipped coffee in front of a blue-flamed driftwood fire. "Why did you marry me and what happened to us? I got lost somewhere along the way."

They had not touched each other except for that first time back at the cottage, but she felt curiously more at ease with him than she could remember feeling with anyone for a long time. She hadn't even wondered at his sudden appearance after having left him on Cozumel, but Marcus had explained the hastily arranged flight in the Kleins' six-passenger jet. He had actually arrived hours before she had and had been anxiously awaiting her.

Marcus sat silent for a few moments. The light from the parchment-shaded lamp highlighted her sharply defined cheekbones and cast into shadow her deep-set eyes.

"Kendrik, I've told you a little about myself. Probably more than I've ever told anyone else, as a matter of fact, but there are still things to be cleared up. You're familiar with the work I'm doing on the book, and it's pretty much the sort of thing I've done for years—well, two or three years, at least." He grinned wryly. "There was a time when I lived a different sort of life. Money was never a problem, or rather, a lack of it wasn't. After a while, though, I began to wonder if I wasn't missing something of value. It occurred to me that anything that could be bought could easily be lost—and that included most of my friends. Most of them dropped out of the picture when I started digging into work and quit the night life and resort rounds. Erma and Sheila stuck longer—couldn't believe the leopard had really changed his spots, I guess. Anyhow, I didn't have a whole lot of faith in the goodness of mankind, in marriage or—love."

He raised his eyes, and they seemed to see all the way into Kendrik's soul. "It took a kid, a green-eyed witch who got under my skin before I knew what was happening, to straighten me out. Sweetheart"—he looked as nearly vulnerable as a man of Marcus's stature can be—"I don't know why you married me. Infatuation, security, whatever reasons a young girl has for marrying a man my age."

"I married you because I—" she began, but he put his finger against her lips.

"Darling, whatever it is, it's all right. I know you didn't even know about the money. Even if I hadn't heard that from Mara, I'd already drawn my own conclusions. Erma did her damnedest to stir up suspicion, but I was already getting to know you then. I'm afraid she picked up some information from Vonnie or Nina or someone and passed it on to you with her own wicked twist added just when we got married, didn't she?"

Kendrik nodded, then asked, "But why did you act as if you hated me so much of the time? And then you followed me home. Why? Oh, Marcus—I wanted you to, but I thought you'd be glad I was gone. I thought you wanted Mitzi—and Erma."

"Oh, my little goose! Don't you know the world is full of Mitzis and Ermas—and Scott Chandlers, too?" He quirked a brow at her, and she caught the gleam of humor in his eyes. "I was trying to shake you loose, honey. I knew there had been something there, something special and wonderful that somehow got lost along the way. I wanted to get under your skin and find out what had happened to you! Make you react, commit yourself! Instead, every time I got close to you, either you froze up or we were interrupted. I was at the end of my rope, sleeping in the same room with you—once even in the same bed!"

"Then it wasn't just a dream? You really did—did?"

"Yes, honey, I really did—did. I held your shivering little body to keep you warm and recited the multiplication tables, the Twenty-third Psalm, and all of Shakespeare I could recall!"

He grinned at her, then his eyes became serious. "Kendrik, if you have any doubts, you'd better speak up now. I fought a good fight against getting involved, getting tied down, and I'm not sure whether I won or lost. All I know is, you're my wife, and we're going to be together from now on, either here on the island or wherever I get sent on roving commissions. I don't think I stood a chance from the beginning. Nor did you, if you'll admit it, my wicked witch of the east!" He leaned closer, and Kendrik caught her breath at the wonder of what she saw in his eyes.

Her voice was scarcely audible as she brought forth her last remaining doubt for examination. "Marcus, what about Erma? She said that you—you married me because I had trapped you, that Buck and the fishermen had seen us together at your house before daylight and—" Her eyes fell before his.

"Oh, precious!" He gathered her close to him, resting his face against her hair. "I've behaved brutally toward you in the past, haven't I? Erma never meant anything to me. No one did until you came along. I guess that was why I resisted your efforts to tame me for so long. I didn't trust the tenderer emotions."

He held her away and grinned down at her, lightly kissing the tip of her nose. "How did you ever manage to dig in under this tough old hide of mine and get yourself embedded in my heart, hmmm? Matter of fact, it was the fact that Buck and the others might have seen you that tipped me off to how much I was beginning to care for you. The very thought of anyone's malice or slander touching you, hurting you, made me realize that I wanted to take care of you more than anything else in the world. That was something totally new to me, sweetheart." His words were unbelievably soft, and Kendrik felt her bones turn to honey, her eyelids grow heavy.

Outside, the rain had set in for forever, and an early gloom pervaded the warm intimate room. The language of love knows no boundaries of time or space, and it could have been hours or only minutes later that Kendrik stirred in her husband's arms.

"Marcus ... darling?"

"Hmmmm?"

"That trunk, is it still here?"

"Yep."

"What do you suppose is in it?"

"Nothing."

"Nothing! What do you mean?" She sat up, looking down at the flickering firelight on his rugged features.

"Just what I said. Nothing." Really, his smile was unbelievably smug.

"But how do you know?"

"I looked in it as soon as I found out who it belonged to."

"But why didn't you tell me? Why all the trips back and forth about an empty old trunk?" she demanded, puzzled.

"Do I tell a trout that there's no nourishment to be had at the end of my flyrod? Now, don't be silly! Come on back down here where you belong."